Praise for Eli.

The Winds of Fate Reviews:
myBook.to/TheWindsofFate

> *The Winds of Fate* "...captivating romance that takes us to the world of seventeenth-century London... Sexual tension and legal and familial intrigue ensue with the reader cheering on the lovely pair."

> <u>**—Publishers Weekly**</u>

> *The Winds of Fate* "has everything...full of passion, betrayal, mystery and all the good stuff readers love."

> <u>**—ABNA Reviewer**</u>

> "Original...strong-willed heroine...I love all of it...the unlikely premise of a female member of the aristocracy visiting a man who is condemned to die and asking him to marry her."

> <u>**—ABNA Reviewer**</u>

Surrender the Wind Reviews:
http://hyperurl.co/qnu96k

Surrender the Wind "The lush descriptions of the southern countryside, the witty repartee between the characters, the factual descriptions of battles woven into the storylines, and the rich characters kept me glued to the pages."

—Alwyztrouble's Romance Reviews

Surrender the Wind received the "Crowned Heart" and National "RONE AWARD" finalist for excellence. "With twists and turns…and several related subplots woven in, no emotional stone is left unturned in this romance."

—InD'tale Magazine

Light of My Heart

DUKE OF RUTLAND SERIES BOOK II

Elizabeth St. Michel

Light of My Heart by Elizabeth St. Michel. Copyright © 2017R. All rights presently reserved by the author. Printed in the United States of America. No part of this book may be used or reproduced in any manner whatsoever without written permission except in the case of brief quotations embodied in critical articles or reviews.

This novel is a work of fiction. Names, characters, places and incidents are either products of the author's imagination or used fictitiously. Any resemblance to actual events, locales, or persons, living or dead, is entirely coincidental. All rights reserved. No part of this publication can be reproduced or transmitted in any form or by any means, electronic or mechanical, without permission in writing from Elizabeth St. Michel.

Library of Congress Catalog Number: 2017910429
ISBN: 0997482443
ISBN: 9780997482447

For my children,
Edward, Michael, Stephanie, Christine and Matthew
You've been a blessing from the start.
I love you with all my heart.

Chapter 1

Leicestershire, England 1779

*A*nthony Rutland hated being late as much as he loathed disorder. He rounded the arborvitae hedgerow bordering his laboratory. The door banged open in the wind. A vein pulsed in his neck. Other than his lab assistant, George, who had been missing for three days, no one dared to cross the threshold. An intruder? There had been problems in the past with unknown enemies of the Rutland family. Flasks banged. Burettes clinked. The intruder was not concerned about making noise.

George would never be so careless. Although lackluster in aptitude, the man understood Anthony's perfectionism in maintaining the lab's organization and was the only assistant who had stayed with him for more than six months. Since George's absence, Anthony's lab mushroomed into chaos. Given that his assistant was not the kind to venture off, a niggling crept up his spine. He clenched his hand. To put his fist through someone's face appealed. The velocity, the impact of that collision, and then the end result to his hand would no doubt present an exercise in futility and would further delay his entrance into the Royal Society of Science for ungentlemanly behavior.

Anthony entered his inner sanctum. His eyes widened. The most exquisite woman he'd ever seen stood in a triangle of light, washing his lab equipment. His breath stalled, and for a moment he couldn't breathe. He assessed the statistical odds that nature could improve upon perfection. None.

What must have been five pounds of wild, rich auburn hair was swept atop her in a gentle swirl and cascaded in a mass of loose ringlets. Errant tendrils escaped and he found that flaw enhanced what nature had delivered. Her nose was straight, delicately boned, and her skin was pinkened by the sun—as if the girl cared more for health than a fashionably pale complexion.

She stretched, reached back, massaging her spine. The outline of rounded breasts strained heavily against silk, the effect more than a simple provocation and yielded an act of war on his senses. His anatomy, like a compass, pointed stiffly north. What was the likelihood of his physical reaction? *If probability equals one, an event will almost occur and definitely had occurred.*

Females rarely captured his attention, even his late wife whom he had married out of duty had failed to hold his interest. He had not loved her, didn't know if he was capable of that emotion. Celeste had been skittish and had begged to postpone their wedding night. Too involved in his work, Anthony had honored her request. The marriage lasted two weeks before she broke her neck. If he had spent more time with her...she'd be alive. For four years he wrestled with the guilt for not protecting his wife.

He had tried to blend into the world and the disappointment of attempting to mix into humanity yielded a terrifying reality. He was doomed to be alone in the universe. He cultivated that loneliness, night and day immersed in his work, allowing the loneliness to tunnel into his soul. Long ago, he had given up hope of finding someone who would understand him, someone to fill that space. Unlike his brothers, who had dallied with women, Anthony lost himself in his lust for science and discovery. Not that an impudent maid hadn't thrown herself at him, but at thirty years of age, he was burdened with an unhappy consequence. He was a virgin.

But now with a complete stranger, all manner of wicked thoughts filled his brain. Would her hair feel soft and silky in his fingers, would her lips yield willingly under his, would she... He shook his head. How absurd? He was a scientist, not a randy adolescent boy.

Bottles straight, counters wiped, his lab had been cleaned, polished and organized. Never before had he seen such industry even in the best of his lab assistants. With reverence she employed a feather duster, her hands, dictating a soft swish over glass bottles. How would those same hands feel stroking his body? Where did that idea come from? She picked up a notebook. Humming a tune while she read, the vibrations from her vocal cords radiated a soft moan of pleasure and desire that flowed over him like rich warm cream. He could watch her thumb through the pages all day.

Reading? Like a condor off the Pyrenees, Anthony swooped down and slammed his notebook shut. "How dare you read my private notes?"

Her hand flew to her chest, knocking a bottle off the cabinet. Glass shattered and splintered. She stooped to pick up the pieces. "I'm so sorry."

"That was one of my most expensive Flemish flasks," he growled, hovering over the woman. Her creamy skin reddened. He clenched his jaw. Wasn't her fault he couldn't get a grip on his lust.

"You don't have to gnash your teeth. I was trying to help," she said.

Her accent was unusual, clipped, and wild. Definitely American, a Yank. Her unfortunate circumstance was her place of birth. He couldn't hold her place of birth against her. Weren't all Americans an unruly, boorish lot with minimal education and un-refined thinking? "It will be months and costly to replace, not to mention that I need it now."

"I will pay for it."

Her voice, soft yet defiant, robbed him of his anger. He raked his fingers through his hair. He was a brute, knew it, but was unable to erase the unease over his absent assistant, and further, why was a Colonial woman… "Who gave you permission to enter my laboratory?"

"Your father."

Did her chin actually lift a notch? "My father would never—"

"I did," the duke answered, his words slow and meticulous as he strolled in and sat on a stool. His posture translated serious business.

When was the last time his father had turned up in his laboratory?

"Anthony, this is Miss Rachel Thorne from Boston," said the duke. "I would have escorted Miss Thorne, but I had some last minute business to attend and told her to meet me here. Your sister, Abby has sent Rachel for us to introduce to society."

Anthony had forgotten the arrangement made months ago. Rachel was cousin to the notorious American privateer, Captain Jacob Thorne who had rescued Abby from a kidnapping. They had fallen in love, married, and now lived in Boston with their infant son. With the war against the Colonies still raging, and Miss Thorne's relationship to enemies of the Crown, finding her a husband in English society wouldn't— He pulled back his shoulders. Good God, why didn't she simply marry someone in the Colonies?

"What does this have to do with me?"

The duke gave a stern eye that brooked no disagreement. "You will be her escort along with Lady March until other arrangements can be made."

"Impossible. A waste of my valuable time and with my assistant unaccounted for. . ."

"He doesn't have to escort me," announced the author of his imminent imprisonment.

She walked past him, the sway of hips and soft swish of her skirts mesmerized him. Good Lord, the woman possessed weapons enough to scorch his backside.

The duke thumped his silver-headed cane on the floor. "Yes, he does. He will accompany you to dinners, balls, whatever invitations you receive, instead of maintaining his hermit-like existence."

Anthony swept his arm over his laboratory. "I have a myriad of experiments to complete and lacking competent help, the likelihood of any one of them being achieved is hopeless."

His father's lips formed a stiff line. Anthony was accustomed to applying carefully constructed scientific methods and planned his life accordingly, but this particular scenario had disintegrated into madness, and his father, the duke had taken on the role as director.

"You have it all wrong." She raised her chin and looked down her nose at Anthony.

The hackles rose on his neck.

Anthony crossed his arms. "What do I have wrong?"

"Your formula on hydraulics is full of errors."

Anthony snorted. "Did I hear you right?" The prospect of a woman having an idea of modern hydraulics was laughable. He grabbed his notebook and flicked through the pages. He knew exactly to what she insinuated.

She marched to the cabinet, shoulder to shoulder with him. To ignore her height, he focused his gaze on his notes. Was it lavender or lemon balm that entwined him? She snatched a quill and scratched on a sheet of paper. "This is the way your calculations should read."

"If you say so." There was not a prayer her computations would be accurate. Impossible for a Colonial woman to have the least idea of force, pressure and area of liquids. For weeks, he had suffered with the formula. He compared his calculations to... His mouth fell open. By God, what she had assessed in minutes made complete sense. Brilliant. "How do you know this?"

"It is a hobby of mine."

"Hobby? This knowledge takes years...we need to discuss this."

"You have booted me from your lab. Remember? And refused to be my escort."

The duke rose and took her by the arm. "Miss Thorne will be occupied today. The seamstresses are waiting for her fittings."

The Colonial woman halted. "Fittings? I couldn't possibly—"

The duke put his hand up. "My daughter is three thousand miles away and I miss her terribly. By way of her letters, Abby has ordered a new wardrobe for you. I will honor her request."

Anthony tossed his notes aside. "She can't go. I must have more conversation—"

Miss Thorne paused with a dismissive glance over her shoulder. "Are we having a conversation? If there were a hanging for hospitality, Lord Anthony, you'd be last in line. I wouldn't dream of wasting your time."

Chapter 2

*R*achel prided herself on…people's predictability. She sighed. Except nothing about Lord Anthony Rutland was predictable. To think he was privy to all the secrets of the universe. How good it was to show him he was wrong. Let him chew on that for a while.

This is taking too long. Standing on top of a stool with an army of pin-sticking dressmakers making endless adjustments made her head ache. Rachel had argued that her own family could well afford the gowns, but the duke remained unyielding, forcing her to relent.

Over the past year, she and Abby had become like sisters, confiding the deepest of secrets. Rachel had revealed to Abby her near rape by an English officer during the British occupation of Boston and the unbearable yoke of the stigma attached to her assumed defilement. Boston was a small town and news had traveled like fire through kindling. Despite her innocence, and even with the family's efforts to rectify the dilemma, salacious gossip damned her. When suitors disappeared, she knew why. Rachel swallowed feelings of unworthiness. No man of any value would want her. Abby had insisted on a visit to her ancestral home outside London where Rachel could have a fresh start without the taint of disgrace attached to her. She had entered the country through a different port with a contrived story of her loyalist leanings.

How she'd rather be in that marvelous laboratory. The joy of being present there this morning, all the equipment and outfittings laid before her. That rich sensual feel of discovery at her fingertips. For months she had dreamed of seeing the newly built laboratory that Abby had described via letters from her father. Flowing through her veins was the love and enthusiasm of science, direct, simple and passionate. Never could she get enough. When she was discovering, she was unchained, free from the torment of her muddled past.

Abby had talked about her older brother, Anthony and his experiments with electricity. A whole new world dawned and Rachel had created with her heart, and built with her mind, an image of him. She ground her teeth. Lord Anthony. He had spoiled everything. Abby didn't know her brother at all. He was not the sweet conscientious man Abby had portrayed. More like Attila the Hun.

"Ouch." A pin skewered Rachel, punishing her for her woolgathering.

"My apologies," said the dressmaker and showered upon Rachel a myriad of fabrics to choose, satin, bombazine, velvet, silk and taffetas in a dazzling array of reds, golds and sapphires.

Her skin tingled with the unexpected. Lord Anthony was as elemental as the changing universe, uncontrolled energy, with nothing lagging or degenerated about him—no softness at all to his solid and imposing frame.

Trimmings of ribbons, Chantilly lace, seed pearls and ostrich feathers were held up to taunt her. "Good Lord, what would I need with ostrich feathers?"

"For your riding habit hat," the dressmaker explained, all but rubbing her hands with glee, the subtle suggestions drawing upon a tenacious campaign that such extravagant dealing implied. The duke had given orders to spare no expense. There was the matter of the dinner party this evening that Rachel must attend and a new dress must be readied for the event. With certainty, there would be a sizeable recompense for such a feat. The dressmaker would likely swoon at the amount of profits she would make from the necessary gowns, undergarments, and clothing items.

Abby had not warned Rachel of how devastatingly handsome her brother was. His eyes were baffling shades of blue, like lapis intershot with sunshine—dark, light, bluish grey, and intermittently, the azure of a stormy sea. Indeed, he had arrested her attention. Hadn't he arched a dark brow and stared at her until she felt ready to squirm? His shirt had been askew and most charming, as if he had more important matters in the world to attend than an immaculate appearance. Her heart shuddered, stopping for a moment, and then began beating anew at a frantic pace. She didn't know what emotion it was he caused to rise within her. Fear? No. She did not fear him.

Rachel tapped a finger on her lips. Admiration. That was it. Paging through his notes, she had discovered a genius. He dabbled in everything in the physical and biological world, extensive diagrams and formulas, theories and postulations. Did his mind ever rest?

"Let me get the other fabrics I brought for you to consider." The dressmaker departed for the adjacent room which no doubt housed a repository of fabric.

Rachel's back ached and a chill set across her body from the long hours of standing in nothing but her chemise and a half-sewn dress.

Anthony walked in and barreled right toward her. "I've been thinking about the formula you left me and I need to—"

Rachel crossed her arms over her chest. She blushed from the tips of her toes to the roots of her hair. The seamstresses squealed. From the uproar, the dressmaker returned and frosted their intruder with a withering stare. "Lord Anthony!"

At her icy authority, Anthony stepped back. He frowned, looking Rachel up and down. Thunderstruck, his jaw dropped with the dawning realization of her dishabille and his indiscretion. "My apologies."

The dressmaker slammed the door in his face. When Rachel's lightheadedness diminished, she gave a small smile. Poor Anthony. She had baited and whetted his appetite with the hydraulic formula on incompressible flows. Of course, he'd be like a dog after a bone until he obtained more answers.

Predictable.

Chapter 3

*A*nthony scowled. He knew exactly what Miss Thorne was doing, making him cool his heels through fittings, a nap, her toilette. He had received a note from her, informing him that Lord Humphrey, her cousin Jacob's half-brother, had offered to be her escort this evening, relieving Anthony of his duty. Time had completely gotten away from Anthony and he was arriving at Chelmsford's home at the eleventh hour. He scaled the steps, tossed his hat and coat to the awaiting footman.

Already seated at the dinner table, pink-cheeked and smiling, was Miss Thorne, like a flower among weeds. The blue dress she wore, miraculously prepared by the seamstresses this afternoon, molded snugly to her narrow waist. Her breasts pushed high enough to spill impressively over the bodice. On any other woman the gown would be lackluster, but on Rachel, the gown evoked a time-less elegance, like a mathematical theorem exactly proportional to a number of independent ideas he could grasp in a theorem, and inversely proportional to the endeavor it took to envisage them. In spite of Anthony's astonishment, it was difficult to believe she was the same outlandish woman who had invaded his laboratory, and then dared to keep him at bay all afternoon.

Anthony nodded to Lord Humphrey and Lady March. The rest of the fifty inhabitants he could care less about. Rachel finished an anecdote and pure energy boomed around her, a tangible throb of laughter.

He was seated in the only chair left across from her. "Miss Thorne, I'd like to continue our discussion." His request came out as a command and she straightened.

"Enjoy the party," said his host, Lord Chelmsford. Chelmsford, his former roommate at Eton had a predilection for taverns, billiard rooms and other forbidden premises. Where Anthony excelled and prodigiously graduated in two years before attending Oxford, Chelmsford barely finished Eton at four years, no doubt earning his degree in buffoonery. Time had not altered him.

"Shocked to see you. Thought you'd fallen off the edge of the world," said Chelmsford.

Anthony ignored him. "About the hydraulic—"

Miss Thorne sighed, her eyes, though a gentle blue, seemed unusually penetrating, as if they had witnessed a profundity of experience seldom met by a person her age.

"You should have learned patience, Lord Anthony. It's a conquering virtue."

"There's no time for it." Right now, he was a highly combustible, biological and chemical compound ready to explode. "Unless you really don't know." *Take that, Miss Thorne.* With certainty, she'd submit to thumbscrews before she let him have the upper hand.

She disentangled herself from her partner's conversation and smiled at him impudently. Wisely, Anthony restrained himself from grinning outright. It wouldn't do to send Miss Thorne into a temper. Beneath that angelic expression, her eyes glittered then darkened, and then with a momentary flash, bore through him for revealing her as a bluestocking.

"Drawing upon Sir Isaac Newton's laws of motion and laws of viscosity—" she said, "—I implemented Bernoulli's Calculus that affirms for an inviscid flow of a non-conducting fluid. An increase in the speed of the fluid occurs simultaneously with a decrease in pressure or a decrease in the fluid's potential energy."

Everyone turned and stared. A woman having intellectual interests? Anthony did not care. It was in the interest of science. "I had rejected Bernoulli in my calculations."

"Your error, Lord Anthony. You need to move from Pascal." She inclined her head, a candid censure, indicating he was using calculus from an earlier mathematician.

"Amazing," said Lord Robert Ward, his guttural voice grating, as if he worked in a coalmine and swallowed dust. "Didn't know you made errors, Rutland."

A vein pulsed at the base of Anthony's throat while Lord Ward did a double take, his gaze making a slow motion trail from Miss Thorne's face down to her bodice. Hot blood shot through Anthony's veins. How long would it take for a two hundred and thirty-five-pound man to dissolve in a vat of sulfuric acid? One day? Two days?

Lord Ward had already gained entrance to the coveted Royal Society of Science. Of course, from the notes on electricity he had paid someone to steal from Anthony's laboratory a year ago.

His hands fisted. Oh, what he would like to do to...could do...

At the age of nine, Anthony's older brother, Nicolas had insisted on boxing lessons for the two of them. At first, Anthony had seen the sport as transitory but the exercise proved to give him satisfaction and kept him in shape. He sparred with the tenants on his father's estate, massive farm boys built from hardened work, eager to take on the duke's son with no regard for his position. The fighting was dirty, and he liked it that way.

Anthony focused his gaze on his nemesis. "So nice to see you, Ward. Your presence, like an indefinite visit from an impossible senior relative, with all the dottiness, fragility of mind, and...terrible thievery. When you leave, no one will shed tears of sadness, on the contrary, tears of relief."

"Are you questioning my honor?"

"I am not questioning your honor; I am denying its existence."

"I could call you out for that," Ward snarled.

"You wouldn't. You're a terrible shot, couldn't hit the broadside of His Majesty's ship."

"Lord Anthony, have you finished your electrical experiments? Of course, your paradigm is a little off, but I understand your lacking—" smirked Ward as if he knew so much more.

The more was what Lord Ward had stolen from him. In hindsight, Anthony now stored many of his notes in his head in case Lord Ward attempted to steal from him again.

"Lord Rutland has astounding aptitude in his study of electricity," said Miss Thorne.

"Do tell, Miss Thorne," lured Lord Ward.

Anthony narrowed his eyes. How much had she read of his notes? She had no idea that Ward was trying to steal his work again.

"Enough to say his genius is incomparable."

Anthony lifted a brow. Why had she championed him when he had tainted her with a wolfish intellectual passion so unlike her sex? Ward snorted. "And you can say this because—"

"Because I have followed Dr. Benjamin Franklin's discoveries and have had a look at Lord Anthony's notes."

Ward leaned over the table to assign a confidential tone, yet spoke loud enough over the hushed whispers and watchful eyes for all to gather what he'd said. His hard blue eyes stared across the table to Lord Anthony. "You compare Lord Anthony to Dr. Franklin?"

"I do. Dr. Franklin is mortal. Lord Anthony is supernatural."

"So much knowledge for a Colonial woman?" Lord Ward jeered, then looked down her bodice.

Although giving a brilliant smile, Miss Thorne's eyes narrowed as she locked gazes with Lord Ward. "With what part do you have the most difficulty? The fact I'm a Colonial…or that I'm a woman? Either of which I consider high praise. I dare say that you could not beat Lord Anthony in any one of the electrical discoveries that he is about to launch."

Anthony ground his teeth. She had thrown down the gauntlet. No way did he have even one of his experiments close to completion. To wring her neck.

Lord Ward's mouth opened and closed a couple of times before he sputtered, "You dare to make such a declaration?"

"Afraid?" Anthony made a broad sweep of his arm. He had enough of Ward's eyeing Miss Thorne's charms. "Be aware, I ask politely only once, after that, I'll not be called a fool. There are many invited guests to witness the challenge. So you see, prudence suggests that we make amends, steel our soft hearts to the inevitable, and invite you to be so accommodating to answer the contest."

"I see," said Ward with mock-urbanity and suave detachment, waving an effeminate hand while taking his measure of Lord Anthony. "I confess there is much force in what you say."

"It's with good cheer that you lighten my sentiments," said Anthony. "If I win, I will take your position at the Royal Society of Science, and if you win, Lord Ward, I will forfeit five thousand pounds."

Ward's eyes played over Anthony like points of steel. "Never will I lose, so get used to being five thousand pounds lighter in the pocket."

He smiled at the pompous man. "Then allow me to put it another way—perhaps more indulgent. I will have what is mine by rights. This I do not doubt."

Murmurs of shock mounted around the table from the unorthodox gambit but Anthony had his eyes fixed on Lord Ward. If the fraud had a gun, Anthony would have a bullet in the head.

Dinner ended, the men stood and before the ladies left for the drawing room, he felt *her* presence next to him. Her hand threaded through his arm, warm and delicious. He looked down on her and she smiled up to him.

She drew her hand away as if she were too forward. He recaptured her hand and placed it on his arm, patted it, and held her beside him. Which of them trembled?

"Lord Anthony, I am weary from my travels. Do you think you could escort me home?"

His heart slammed against his chest. How could he resist? He told Lady March, Rachel's chaperone to bid adieu to her friends and to meet them at the entrance. He said good night to Lord Chelmsford and felt no remorse, informing a disappointed Lord Humphrey that he was escorting Miss Thorne home. He collected their hats and cloaks and they waited on the outdoor steps of Chelmsford's home for the Rutland coach to pull up from a collection of carriages.

Her vexing wager rattled in his head. "Look at the fine conundrum you've got me into. I'm nowhere near your cock-and-bull story. I'll be the laughing stock of England."

She withdrew her hand. He snatched it back and held it on his arm, unable to define the warmth radiating inside him, despite his consternation. Her hand felt at home there.

Her lips parted, surprised by the gesture as much as he. "I should be the one angry with you for exposing my accomplishments, but Lord Ward needed a reprimand. He insulted you and I took exception. What else was I to do?"

"You should have consulted me first." A cold wind pushed against his jacket, the kind that numbed the lips and froze the face. She automatically leaned into him, poaching his warmth. "This morning—" he said. "—I paid a visit to my assistant's brother to confirm he had never returned home. I don't have a good feeling, and worry that something nefarious has happened to George. I need him. Without another pair of hands, my work will be as slow as a broken-winded, hobbled mare."

Drizzle fell sluggishly down, and the air felt cold and clammy. Rachel ducked further into her cape. "I'll be your assistant."

"You?"

Her breath came out in a puff of fog. "I'm more than qualified. I read at the age of three and have had a lifelong love of science."

He heard the jingle of reins and a coachman's sharp whistle to halt the carriage horses. "I suppose you are going to tell me you sat on the same rock as Dr. Franklin."

She bobbed up on her toes, her eyes meeting his. "We are friends. When I was thirteen, I met him in Philadelphia. Ever since, I've been cursed with the love of electricity and its workings. We correspond regularly."

"Then I shall require your help in the laboratory——" Anthony might have been enraptured with the soft dreaminess in her blue eyes except three things happened in neat deadly preordained rhythm, as slow as the tick of a Huygens clock. The pendulum shortened, the swing of the arc reduced, *one, and two, and three.* A flash of light from a balcony up above, a harsh laugh, and a scraping of something heavy being moved.

Instinct or his systematic mind made him look up. Like a bullet, he grabbed Rachel and used his body to curl around her, pitching her over the steps and into the bushes. A concrete flower pot exploded on the top of the steps right where they had been standing. He had used his body to cushion the fall, Miss Thorne sprawled on top of him, her hat gone, her rich auburn hair unpinned and flowing over him. Besides the barberry thorns stuck into his back he warmed, very comfortable with her on top of him.

She curved her hand on the side of his face. "You saved my life."

A whole world of complexities pulled his heart away from the gloom where he had not been able to save his wife's life. *You saved my life*. Rachel's words, thrown in so much loneliness was like a hand pulling him out of the quicksand, scooping him up from a place of drowning and into the wild richness of air. She was breathing hard. Anthony didn't know whether to kiss her or expound on the gravitational pull and impact of a one hundred-pound mass on two biological bodies...and the likelihood of survival. The latter was safer.

"My hat."

"We've averted near death and you are worried about your hat?"

She scrambled off him, stood on shaky limbs, then plunged through the shrubs. "Lord Rutland, there is a man. I think he is dead."

Grooms quickly gathered from the carriages parked in the circular driveway. Anthony ordered the Rutland head coachman to hold up a lantern while he parted a bush. His breath hitched. George lay with a large bloody gash across his head and a pool of blood saturated the ground. A sudden coldness hit Anthony's core. He reached to his assistant's neck, felt for a pulse. Nothing. He was dead.

Anthony took off his coat and covered his assistant. His voice broke with the horrific death George had faced. "Get the authorities," he ordered one of the grooms. George died because he worked for Anthony.

He turned to Miss Thorne, scrubbed a hand over his face. "My assistant, George. Whatever twisted mind did this, sent a message loud and clear. I will notify his family."

Chapter 4

After spending half of the night at the Duke of Chelmsford's with the authorities, Rachel now sat in the library of Anthony's ancestral home for further examination of George's terrible demise. Lady Ward had retired from all the excitement of the evening. Rachel had changed out of her silk gown and rested on a brocade chair opposite Anthony.

A fire crackled in the fireplace, warding off the damp winter chill and illuminating a vast number of leather bound books that populated the shelves from the floor to the gallery above. How she itched to read every tome and how lucky Anthony was to live in a scholarly paradise.

Anthony sans his frockcoat, leaned forward, rested his elbow on his knees, easy in his skin, yet attentive. His ebony hair, pulled back in a queue, fell over his snowy white shirt. Other than a tear in his stocking there was no evidence of their fall into the barberry bushes. Her face heated from the memory of that awkward position. She tilted her head to the ceiling of gilded stucco, that presented framed paintings of God, angels in war, and the seizure of earthly mortals from demons below.

Anthony caught her staring at the motif, his deep baritone voice infused with shades of deeper meaning. "The artist demonstrated the deadly poison of the serpent destroyed by joy that filled the souls of the vanquished and served the power of redemption."

How wonderful he was to distract her for a moment from the night's events. Not to be outdone, she said, "The artist has captured the iron hand of right and absolute, yielding a stronger force that defeats evil and allows us to move from darkness to light." As she parlayed the response, a lightness tingled in her chest, enjoying the shared intellectual camaraderie. *Touché, Lord Anthony.*

Anthony pressed his lips together. "Or has the artist divined the experiences of our past are the architects of our present?"

She could not think of one thing to counter his debate, not when she swiped a tiny rapier and Lord Anthony served a blow with a battle-axe. *I will win next time.* Rachel smiled and for a moment, the embossed tomes, the beeswax candles sputtering in candelabras, and then the walls, melted away. The world, and all its inherent drama, vanished leaving only the two of them, and an intangible profoundness that left them intimately connected.

Catching her breath, Rachel ripped her stare from Anthony's compelling regard, thankful for the interruption of Duke Richard Rutland's entrance and trailed by a servant carrying tray of food. The servant poured tea and following the Duke's nod, departed, closing the doors behind him with a light snap.

Duke Richard Rutland stared out the heavily draped windows. His silence loomed. He was a tall, handsome, imposing man, regal with dark hair greying at his temples, and smartly dressed despite the lateness of the hour. He did not have the thickening middle that a man his age would present. No. He was rather robust and appeared as one who rode horses for hours, and...he was forbidding. His staunch demeanor gave the appearance of someone you'd dare not cross.

The Duke sat behind his massive rosewood desk. "I wanted to talk to the two of you without the authorities. There is more to George's death and the attempt on your lives this evening. We've been lax since Nicolas and Abby's kidnapping a year ago. Again, we are being played upon by an unseen adversary."

Anthony rubbed his thumb across his chiseled jaw. "I remember the whole situation as if it happened yesterday. During Abby's betrothal party, both father and I had received a life and death summons to my laboratory."

Duke Richard threaded his fingers through his hair. "Fortunately, my impatient nature saved us. For I believed a hoax had been played and we left, seconds before the lab exploded. During the chaos, Abby had been abducted by Percy Devol, a madman bent on revenge against the long deceased Duke of Rutland, Anthony's grandfather, holding the insane and illogical belief that he was the rightful heir to the dukedom. His goal had been to eliminate all of the Rutlands."

Anthony stood, strode to a sideboard and poured himself a drink. "Imprisoned aboard the *Civis,* Abby would have perished under the thumb of the ship's Captain, a former slaver, and his dreadful crew if not for your cousin, Jacob Thorne. Fortunately, his privateering activities included capturing the merchantman in which Abby was held prisoner."

Anthony picked up his drink and tossed it back with a single swallow. "Our enemies were clever during the orchestrated disorder. My oldest brother, Nicolas and heir and had been captured and locked away on a Portuguese slaver bound for Brazil where he was meant to die enslaved in back-breaking labor beneath the hot tropical sun. His ship never reached Brazil."

The duke spun a crystal paperweight on his desk, seeming absorbed with the activity. Light reflected from candles flashed from the sphere, and disappeared in the shadows. "I received a message today from the King," he said. "One of His Majesty's frigates discovered wreckage in the Caribbean Sea, confirming the ship Nicolas had been imprisoned on was destroyed by a hurricane, and all passengers and crew lost at sea. British Naval ships are scouring the West Indies, in case there may be survivors." The duke paused, pulled in a deep breath, retaining his stoic demeanor. Yet, his voice quivered when he said, "I will not give up on my son until we have combed every corner of the Caribbean."

The duke let go of the paperweight and leaned back in his chair. "Is there anything either of you could add? Some observation of suspicious people at the Chelmsfords? A conversation overheard of anyone who might have been involved with George's murder? I need clues. Anything to stop the rogues who attack and endanger our family."

"I was present the night Percy Devol attempted to kill Abby in Boston," Rachel said. "Devol had admitted there were three more enemies of your family. I would start there. Who would have reason enough to hate and kill the Rutlands?"

The Duke raked his fingers through his hair. "How many times have I gone over that same scenario? How many investigators have I sent out only to return empty-handed?"

Rachel patted her lips with a napkin. "Abby and I concurred that for anyone to take on the Duke of Rutland was sheer insanity. So, the question remains, who has the resources to hire two ships to take both Nicolas and Abby? Not Devol. That alone took money and power."

The Duke aimlessly flipped through a few scattered papers. "I am a member of Parliament. My support of the Duke of Richmond in ending the war with the Colonies has met with defiance and animosity. The war is breaking England's economy sustaining pay for a half-million, soldiers, marines and seamen between the Americas, West Indies and the Mediterranean. As a result, I have cultivated enemies—those who profit from the shameful public expenditure."

Rachel took a sip of tea and placed her cup in the saucer. "Clearly the culprits were intent on making the last of the Rutland lineage suffer. That comes from hatred and that particular emotion comes from fear or a perceived injustice and, perhaps, from something personal."

The Duke of Rutland's eyes narrowed. "Yes. Now our adversaries are emboldened and have moved from their dormancy over the past several months to regroup. Their next line of attack is Anthony, the subsequent heir."

"Do you think it was Lord Robert Ward who pushed the urn on us? I didn't want to bring his name up with the authorities since I'm a Colonial and he is a...Lord of the realm. He was so angry with you, Anthony. Just before the vase fell on us, I heard that same gravely laugh, like he had swallowed his lung."

Anthony's head snapped around, eyes intent on her. "I heard it too and had my suspicions, but there was an octave difference. Beneath Lord Ward's bullish exterior, he is a coward, not a murderer."

Rachel shuddered. "The flower pot was meant to kill you, Lord Anthony."

Anthony returned to the settee, sat back, tension visible in his wide shoulders. "I don't believe the urn was meant to kill me. There are two separate events that must be reviewed. I believe the urn falling on us was orchestrated to propel us into the bushes to discover George's body."

Rachel's fingers fluttered to her chest. "You're right. That means the killer knows you. How you'd react to protect me. The killer, or killers, wanted to show you how vulnerable you are...and that they are watching."

"With certainty, the killer followed my movements. Waited until I was leaving Chelmsford's and then had the audacity to plant George's body there to make his sordid deed public."

"The murderer wants attention. But why kill your assistant?"

"Perhaps George had seen or heard something that he shouldn't have. I had a bad feeling this morning when I received a note from his brother that he had not been home for three days. Not the norm for George's character."

The Duke sighed. "I imagine his brother took the news badly."

"Very badly. I promised I would get to the bottom of this atrocity."

The duke steepled his fingers. "We are to assume that whatever George discovered happened three days ago. Perhaps he came face to face with the criminal set on killing you."

"Ask around, Father. The servants, gardeners, stable boys, visitors? Someone must have seen something around the estate. George was a good-sized man and easily noticed."

"They will strike again. To ferret them out will be another matter. I will hire extra guards to station around your laboratory and the house."

Anthony scoffed, "We cannot live in fear."

"We must be vigilant at all times. I cannot risk losing you, Anthony."

Rachel heard the sad-sweet tone in the Duke's voice, and his love for his son. To have lost his eldest must be crushing to him.

"On another note, I heard of your provocation with Lord Ward." The Duke lifted a knowing brow. "So unlike you."

Anthony stared at his father. "I was justified."

The duke nodded. Rachel could see he would not interfere. The Rutlands were a tight family and loyal to one another.

Beyond the French doors the first fingers of dawn stretched in a brilliant display of lavenders, pinks and golds. When Anthony angled his head to the door, she wrinkled her brow, discerning his mysterious cue. She caught on, and standing, placed her hand over her mouth to stifle a yawn. "I will say good night."

Anthony followed her into the hall. "Would you be willing to help me in the laboratory?"

Ten minutes later, and barely able to tamp down her glee, she met Anthony near the row of arborvitae that bordered his lab. Despite missing a night of sleep, she was ready to plunge into one of his scientific projects. They followed smooth flagstones where moss flowed in between the cracks and feeling soft beneath her slippers.

"Miss Thorne," he said, in just the way his father, the Duke would say her name—evenly and with a slight bow. "Am I to believe that you came to England to see my lab?" The fervent scientist, impassioned discoverer, both vanished in that seasoned gallantry.

"There may be some truth in that assumption." Rachel sighed. "I'm visiting England for three months and desire to make the most of my visit."

"I thought the husband hunt was in your scheme."

"Wrong. Husband hunting was Abby's idea."

"With the war going on in the Colonies, travel must be difficult."

"I will return the same way I came. Lisbon is a neutral port for American ships. My brother, Ethan is scheduled to sail there and meet me." They rounded the tall shrubs, the unusual edifice topped with a ridiculous number of cupolas and towers burst into view.

"What do you think of it?"

She wrapped her cloak tighter around her to ward off the wintry air, half-wishing for the roaring fire in the library and smothered a laugh. "Do you want my honest opinion?"

"That bad?"

"Horrific. What madness did the architects have on their minds? Looks like a wedding cake with swirls of frosting piled to the heavens."

"A culinary confection? That is a new commendation. Absurdity was the ecstasy of the designers, yet I cannot claim ownership to the fanciful design no more than I can complain about the monstrosity. Duke Cornelius Westbrook, a close family friend paid for the laboratory and desired a replica of the famed Palace of Sintra in Portugal with the accompanying turrets and towers."

"But all the pink?"

"Embarrassing. A most unfortunate circumstance was that no one was allowed to see the atrocity until completion. My father has incessant nightmares and has ordered the concealment of the horror from the rest of the world by planting taller arborvitae around the perimeter. When I first laid eyes on the structure I wanted to stab hawthorn spikes through my eyeballs."

Rachel giggled and clapped her hands together to warm them from the cold. "A sense of humor or revenge?"

"Although not related, Duke Cornelius is a like a favorite uncle and has been indispensable to our family for years. When Abby was abducted, he discovered the kidnapper's note in the library and did everything in his power to assist in finding Abby and Nicholas. He insisted on building a new laboratory for me, so I could never offend him for his generosity. I have accepted the grandeur and pretend not to notice every time I walk to the lab."

Anthony held open the door for her to enter. To be alone with Sir Anthony would be considered scandalous. Rachel gave herself a stern shake as she fixed her gaze on the equipment at the back of the room, and willed her shaking legs to carry her all the way, praying she would not break another flask. Since he wasn't bothered by the shocking behavior, she hid her discomfiture behind a prudently arranged mask of calmness as the heels of her boots clipped a sharp echo across the floor. This was in the interest of science after all.

But it just wasn't a scandal that made her stomach quiver. After the attack in Boston, she had been shy of men. One man had tried to kiss her in the garden and she ran from him, vomiting in the bushes. She had locked herself in her room for days, thrown books at the wall and cried into her pillow. Nightmares interrupted her sleep. She swallowed a metallic taste of fear, anything to banish the tragedy from her consciousness.

She glanced up from beneath her lashes, hoping Anthony had not seen her distress. Why was she not afraid of him? *Because he is your best friend's brother...he's family.*

He had changed his clothes. No heavy embroidery or gold braiding was attached to his mode of dress, imparted by most men of his rank who enjoyed excess and personal vanity. No. His taste was simple and modest, yet yielded a sensual elegance from black tight-fitting silk breeches and silk stockings that molded the muscles in his calves. He shrugged off his perfectly tailored coat. Rachel inhaled. Weren't his shoulders wider in his immaculate muslin shirt and cravat? How long before his well-groomed appearance—most likely owed to the precision of his valet—became disordered?

He took her coat, his fingers lingering on her shoulders before placing their coats on a hook. Rachel moved away, noting a room to the right she had not seen before. She blushed when she saw the cot, and then assumed that Lord Anthony worked late into the night or took a nap while waiting on his experiments to complete.

She shifted her gaze away from the cot. "May I have a look at the transcripts of the experiment you propose?"

"Do I have your sworn secrecy?" He held up his notebook like the Holy Grail.

"Abby is like a sister to me. I would never betray her family."

He pulled out a chair for her and slapped down his notebook. She poured through the contents, turning page after page, trying not to focus on Anthony, stationed behind her, reading the text with her…so near that she could feel the warmth of him and breathe the faint whiff of sandalwood. She admired his talent and reports on where he had duplicated many of Dr. Franklin's experiments. She tilted her head up to look at him. "Why do I have the distinct feeling you have many of your notes in your head?"

He flashed a wicked smile.

She smoothed a page in front of her with an unsteady hand, and then positioned a beaker and volumetric flask just so.

"For the exact same reason I challenged Lord Ward last night. Unwittingly, I had hired an assistant who had been employed by Ward. The scoundrel copied pages of my notes and transferred the information to Lord Ward who, in turn, took credit for my work."

She tapped a finger on her lip. "The Royal Society of Science is the coveted prize. That is why we must improve on what you have crafted. To do that I need what is in that head of yours. Care to expound?"

"Dr. Franklin grouped several Leyden jars into what he described as a battery. By multiplying the number of holding vessels, a stronger charge could be stored, and more power would be available on discharge."

"And what do you propose?"

"To make a better battery. To prove that electricity can be generated chemically and to make the battery a continuous and reproducible source of electric current."

Rachel stared at him, completely absorbed, trying to grasp the significance of his genius. "It is insane, Lord Anthony. Impossible. It can't be done."

"I call it the Unicorn."

Rachel let out the breath, Anthony's spell still woven tightly around her. "Because it has never been seen. There have been only short bursts of electricity, nothing consistent." She examined his notes again. "Why saltwater?"

Anthony shrugged as if his genius were no great feat. "Electrical fire loves water, is strongly attracted by it, and they can subsist together. My theory is salt water is added density and greater will be the conduction. I hate to see you caught up in all this nonsense, Miss Thorne. But even more disconcerting, being near me could get you hurt or killed."

He referred to his assistant's murder and the consequences of being associated with the Rutland's. She cocked her head and studied him, regardless of the inappropriateness of it. He was a curious man. A genius, but an enigma. Tall and lean, a day's growth of a beard and brilliant blue eyes, clear as the sky that graced a summer morn. Anthony Rutland was superb. "I'm a big girl. I can take care of myself. Besides you owe me."

"How's that?"

"You saved my life."

She watched his forehead furrow, saw a range of emotion playing across his face, too complex to discern. Guilt? Desperation? Suffering? What? And why? Suddenly she wanted to know everything about him.

He leaned closer, his head dipping down, but his eyes, sincere now, burned at her through dark lashes. His hand hovered in the space between them, his expression a mixture of pain and longing.

Then, as if realizing something, he dropped his hand, his emotion disappearing as swiftly as it had appeared.

He moved away.

Rachel shook her head, unable to dispel the look in his eyes... the despairing, haunted look...as he'd reached toward her. Anthony had scars, hid them well beneath a veneer of isolation. Frightening to be sure, but the naked, yearning, the agony she'd glimpsed painted her unease with bewilderment.

She cleared her throat. "The Chinese believed that through the act of saving someone's life, you are responsible for that life. Since we will be working together, call me, Rachel."

He swung around, dangled his disbelief, left it hanging in the air. "Miss Thorne. That is the most convoluted...you should be indebted to me."

"Rachel." She repeated.

"What?"

"Call me Rachel. While we're working in the lab, call me by my name."

"On one condition, you tell me how a Colonial woman is so well educated?" He handed her a roll of gold foil. "Wrap the gilt paper with the gilt face next to the glass."

He was back to business, shuttered behind his passion for discovery. When she finished the wrapping, she pushed the gilt wrapped jars toward him. "Of course, the brute that you are had to reveal me as a bluestocking at Lord Chelmsford's. I won't forgive you for that. All the tongues will be wagging."

Anthony was standing over her, his hands calmly placing a metal rod through the cork, inserting it into the bottle, not a bit of quiver or restlessness in his hands. She suddenly became aware of how real and large and solid he was and had to force herself to stop squeezing the bottle.

"Since when have I cared about wagging tongues and the rest of humanity? My family and you excluded."

"The rest of humanity? Lord Anthony, you are incorrigible."

"Anthony," he insisted. "Since you are my assistant—"

"Colleague," she corrected and handed him another metal rod to insert in a cork. His mouth closed like he swallowed a cup of vinegar. *Having a hard time with that notion?*

She plunged ahead with her history and education. "An Oxford tutor was supplied to my cousin, Jacob, and my brother, Ethan, with shipments of books from England. Anything required for their education was made available without any knowledge of the benefactor. The tutor noted my capabilities and included me."

Anthony rubbed the back of his neck, bestowing a baleful stare.

Rachel's stomach clenched.

"That doesn't explain the vast extent of your knowledge. Lord Ward was educated in the best of England's institutions. You could have him for breakfast."

Rachel laughed, warming to the subject. "I thank you for the compliment.

"I always tinkered with things, making them better. When my father and Jacob started the shipyard in Boston Harbor, I begged to accompany them and became a regular visitor."

"Your knowledge of hydraulics?"

"I studied the Greeks and Romans, fascinated by the mechanical properties of liquids. I improved on a suction bilge pump, making a double-handled lever, with its fulcrum between the common suction pump. I implemented up-and-down pump handles to drive two pump boxes with two valves in each box that released the water in the bilges and fed the sludge into the sea."

Anthony scoffed. "And you invented this while *tagging along?*"

She moved to the clock on the wall, decorated with a rich Chinoiserie that played a minuet on the quarters of six bells. "Actually…when I ran the shipyard."

Anthony turned his head toward her. "You ran a shipyard?"

She peered through the beveled side glass absorbed with the gears and their workings. "I had to," she said, curling her finger around a tendril of hair and still studying the gears. "This clock is based on Harrison's design."

"And you know that because—"

"Because of the two counterweights at the top of the clock linked by a metal coil in the middle. This is designed to swing back and forth, to act as shock-absorbers against the roll of a ship."

He stopped gathering the jars and gave her his full attention. "Of course, your experience in the shipyard. Harrison designed the clock to take in temperature, humidity, and motion so sailors could calculate longitude with precision. No ship should be without it."

She looked out a front window and caught the yellow gorse and the flattened spiny leaves of Butcher's Broom, lining the lake. "My father died at the Battle of Bunker Hill. My mother followed, dying of influenza, but I believe more from a broken heart from the loss of my father. My brother, Ethan was out privateering. My younger brother, Thomas, died." Her voice caught from the memory of Thomas. "When the British controlled Boston, we suffered the impressment of soldiers in our home." If only Thomas...his senseless death... Guilt, simmered beneath the surface like a capped volcano, unable to erupt. She clutched her heart and tamped down the misery.

Anthony took a step toward her, but stopped when she shook her head.

She didn't want sympathy. Didn't deserve it.

"War broke out and Ethan had been captured and, as far as I knew would breathe his last breath in an English prison. Jacob had been accused of a crime he didn't commit, escaped Boston, and embarked on privateering, raiding the coasts of England. My family had put too much work into the shipyard to let it collapse. I was the only Thorne left. The workers came to me because they didn't want to lose their jobs."

She walked to the sink arrangement and pushed the pump up and down until a spray of water burst out, and then opened the cupboard beneath to investigate the brass piping. "Fascinating to have a pump inside. Brass, too. A fine piece. Guericke's vacuum pump? How deep is the well?"

"I made improvements of Guericke's design. Forty-three feet. I insisted the lab be built over the well. About the shipyard—"

"When the British left Boston, I was commissioned by the Continental Congress, who had authorized the creation of a Continental Navy, to build ships needed to counteract the British naval activities in coastal waters and to facilitate the seizure of commercial and military prizes. So through the encouragement of the workers and Patriots, I managed the shipyard."

"Remarkable." Anthony finished all thirty-five jars, seven rows of five, sealed with a wooden cap and contact wires projected within.

She glanced at him. "I did what I had to do and readily handed over the reins when Jacob returned. The time freed me to work on other interests."

"Electricity."

"Exactly. I was always fascinated when I scuffed my feet over the rug and static fire would appear. After reading Dr. Franklin's notes, I improvised by taking a glass jar with a metal foil cemented to the inside and outside surfaces, and then, projecting a metal terminal vertically through the jar lid to make contact with the inner foil. Like making lightning in a jar." She paused to examine the cluster of jars. "What do you hope to attain by making this series?"

Anthony brushed a wand near the top of the jar, prompting an electrical charge. "You see, the charge passes along the rod and is held within the insulated vessel. Watch when I touch the conducting element to the ends of the rod."

Electrical fire snapped from the device.

"You have stored energy." In a twinkling of the eye, pure energy boomed around them, and Anthony transformed into an eager boy, full of innocent enthusiasm. His excitement was infectious, the pursuit of the unknown and attaining discovery a sphere of activity in which they were permitted to remain children.

She clapped her hands together. Oh, how he made her world full of magic.

When the spark went out, Anthony let out a breath. "It is not good enough. There has to be improvement."

She stroked a gilded jar, her fingers traced the subtle shape of each dip and turn, then rubbed against the thick ridge of the stem. A little purr escaped from her throat and the slight shift of his body caused her to look into deep stormy blue eyes. His pulse throbbed at the base of his throat. The force of his aura crashed through her like an electrical charge. Heart racing, she shifted back a step.

Someone knocked. Anthony opened the door and bade a footman to enter. "His Grace has sent a reminder that it is time to get ready for the ball," he intoned, pivoted and left.

Thank goodness for the distraction. To have a bath. No. To dunk her body in ice-cold water.

"That nonsense. Doesn't he see how important our work is?"

Our. She liked the ring of his opinion. "What time is it? My goodness the whole day has vanished. Maybe it will be good for you to get out and seek entertainment, clear your mind."

"Or clutter it. Nonsense and absurd is the human mating game."

"It can be fun, too," she coaxed.

"I suppose having your teeth pulled is fun."

Rachel moved past him in a swirl of skirts, confining her laughter to a snort. "You have to escort me. It wouldn't be proper otherwise."

"You didn't think about having a proper chaperone once today." Anthony grumbled, the words in him like electricity, dashing itself against glass.

She noted Anthony's scowl. "I did but we are friends. No. More like brother and sister, and this is in the interest of science."

"That's what you call it. Very well, off to the broodmare competition."

"You are terrible."

"I thank *you* for the compliment."

Chapter 5

*A*nthony could not fathom a more hostile environment: a huge, hot press of overdressed giddy people with nothing to do but drink and talk to one another at the top of their lungs with their singular blend of nonsense and idiocy. So full of noise, that the wall of sound blasted enough to make his ears bleed. To lay on a bed of nails for the evening had more appeal.

"I suppose the whirl of silks and satins, the orchestra and so on, must be exciting for you, Miss Thorne." He wrinkled his nose. Women's stale perfume and oceans of flowers exuded a cloying sweetness that testified to the fanciful tendencies and ostentatious taste of their host.

She fanned her face with her hand. "I feel like Cleopatra, out to conquer the world."

His gaze dropped to her lips. "There are other things in the world besides a ridiculous ball. I have long embraced the estimation that the quantity of noise that anyone can tolerate undisturbed survives in inverse proportion to his mental capacity, and consequently viewed as a reasonable good measure of it."

Up close, Miss Thorne was exceptionally beautiful. Best of all was her mouth and her eyes. Together they created a sort of wry, amused liveliness, as if whatever occurred to her, she would remain calm, composed and unruffled through it all, and then she would find some value in it to make her smile.

"You must admit that the ball is thrilling."

He leaned into her, dipped a formal bow. "I get the same thrill a chimney sweep does, shimmying down the chimney into a hot-bed of ashes."

She angled her head up. Her lush mouth mocked him. "We must not squander away life in a small corner of the world. To be nourished with new actions, new aspirations, and new events will lend us new visions."

"More like revelations akin to a rapid current of guests flowing like negative charges into a single room." He spoke to the air as she whirled away with yet another partner.

Lord Humphrey and his father, the Duke of Banfield, moved beside him. Long time neighbors and good friends of the Rutland's, it had always been assumed that Lord Humphrey and his sister, Abby would have married.

"You look bored, Lord Anthony," said Lord Humphrey.

"This is my excited face. You haven't seen bored."

"Miss Thorne presents a picture, don't you think, Lord Anthony?" The Duke of Banfield, pressed on his cane for support. "She hasn't missed one dance."

"Our Miss Thorne is definitely enjoying herself with all her suitors," added Humphrey.

Anthony rolled his shoulders, his frockcoat suddenly tight. *Like dogs after the butcher's cart.*

"I see she is leaving the punch table and being guided out of the ballroom with that rake, Sir Bonneville," said the Duke of Banfield. "Don't you think someone should do something about it?"

Already on the move and cursing under his breath, Anthony stalked after the dandified profligate. He cursed under his breath. Miss Thorne was a naïve Colonial unaccustomed to the nuances of a degenerate like Bonneville. Or was she? He really had no idea of her character. Was she as innocent as he thought? They had vanished. Anthony parted servants in their finest livery and laden with heavy silver trays of wine glasses and appetizers. He searched down one hall, and then another. No doubt, Bonneville dragged her off to the farthest reaches of the house. Standing where one hall met another, he heard Bonneville's wheedling voice.

"Miss Thorne, aren't you the prettiest Colonial I've ever seen."

Anthony's head snapped around, just in time to see Bonneville lead her into the library...away from prying eyes.

Anthony's blood rushed through his veins, pounding against his eardrums like thunder as he loomed in the shadows, his quarry unaware of his existence. Miss Thorne was family. Abby would never forgive him if anything happened to Rachel,

"I'm probably the only Colonial you've ever seen." Her laughter tinkled.

Anthony balled his hands into fists when Bonneville took her cup, gliding his fingers over hers...overlong.

Sir Bonneville shifted toward her, his white complexion stretched tightly over bone, like a corpse bleached in the sun.

"Did I tell you that you have the most beautiful blue eyes?"

Rachel kept stepping back until, finally her shoulders hit the bookcase. "Three times. Once when we were dancing, at the punch table, and now."

"I cannot help it. Your eyes explore my soul and beg my spirit to enter you."

If that wasn't a carnal invite. Bonneville was lint on Anthony's cuff, easy to flick off compared to the farm boys that had honed their skills on him.

"You said there was an original published text in this library by Sir Isaac Newton."

So that was how she was lured by Bonneville. Her voice raised a pitch, her words dagger sharp. Anthony ground his teeth. No one insulted family.

"May I taste your rosebud lips?" prompted Sir Bonneville.

Anthony clenched his fists harder, waiting for her to rebuff the asinine dandy. How good it would feel to release some energy.

"Rosebud lips?" she scoffed. "I have to go." She took a step to move around Bonneville.

Teetering with both cups dangling in his hands, Bonneville sidestepped, blocking her exit. He lowered his head, his sight pinned to her bosom.

Blood shot to Anthony's brain.

He stepped from the shadows and came up next to them. "Is there a problem, Miss Thorne?"

Bonneville twisted his head around and caught Anthony glowering at him that roared, *Steer clear* as obviously as words.

"Lord Anthony, they let you out of your cage? I had the little Colonial first. Move on."

"Miss Thorne is not a piece of property to be claimed."

Jacked-up on sour gin, Bonneville was inspiring. Victory was won by miles but in Bonneville's case it would be inches, as in, how many inches could Anthony slam his fist through Bonneville's face?

"It would be a very rash presumption to think that nowhere else in the cosmos has nature repeated such a strange experiment as your birth, Bonneville."

"You think I'm afraid of you."

"You should be."

"Why? Are you going to zap me with your electrical fire?"

"The idea has merit."

Rachel put her hand on Anthony's arm like a schoolmarm warning a recalcitrant boy. "An incident would be disastrous." She referred to the toll on her reputation. Then there would be the consequences of his father learning of his son's brawling at a ball.

"You're right, Miss Thorne." Anthony offered his arm and turned her toward the exit. She trembled. Fire hardened his muscles and licked through his veins. How he hated Bonneville for putting Rachel in a compromising situation.

Bonneville dared to put a hand on Anthony's shoulder.

Anthony kicked his leg back, at just the right angle, his heel smashed into Bonneville's kneecap with the same thrust he'd use to kick down a stall door. He felt the crack through his boot. Rachel turned and Anthony followed her line of sight, shrugging with innocence. Bonneville was down. In misery. Punch stained his orange en chenille frock coat, breeches, and splattered his cadaverous face. An improvement.

Rachel blinked. "Did you do that on purpose?"

"Do what?"

"Trip him."

"He fell, merely a gravitational force. The punch adds color to his complexion don't you think?"

Her smile made his spirits soar.

"I'm glad you did. I was thinking more of Newton's impulse of force, if extracted and found to be equal to the change in momentum of an object provided the mass is constant. Do we concur that Sir Bonneville's mass is constant?"

Smart girl. They rejoined the Duke of Banfield and Humphrey. A flurry of servants fled down the hall in the direction of the library. The wailing Sir Bonneville had been discovered. No need for any questions. Anthony would deny they were in the library and the Banfield's would back him up—an unwritten code between neighbors who lived side by side for four centuries.

Humphrey grimaced. "Gossip at the ball claims Lord Ward is not going to quit."

As if on cue, Lord Ward and his wife appeared. "Humphrey's right, I'm not quitting."

Anthony scoffed. "Not quitting? You never started. No doubt you'll dazzle us with parlor tricks, hanging orphans from the ceiling and charging them with electricity or shocking dead cats to jump."

Lady Ward worked her fan with the passion of a blacksmith on his bellows. A woman in her thirties, she was beautiful in a hard and glittering manner, except for her ridiculous pouf hairstyle. Indeed, an architectural feat, erected with scaffolding of wire and gauze and covered with fake hair set with flour and lard, and then topped with ostrich feathers. Built so high that Anthony considered how it might interrupt bird migration patterns. He was glad Rachel did not adopt the high powdered fashion and kept the rich glow of her chestnut hair.

"Miss Thorne, I understand you are a Colonial?" Lady Ward's purr was a subtle intimation, connecting Rachel to what was considered the rude and democratic tide that had swept over the Colonies.

"From Boston," Lord Banfield answered for Rachel. "I take your pettiness as a personal affront."

Undeterred, Lady Ward smacked her lips. "Any relation to Captain Thorne?"

"A very distant relation." Anthony cut in, blunt to the point of insult. He would nip Lady Ward's wagging tongue before it had occasion to start.

"But a patriot, everyone must assume." Lady Ward dipped a patronizing smile with the same predatory relish that a vulture shredded carrion with its beak.

Rachel needed his protection, vulnerable to the subtleties of Lady Ward whose personal mission was to vulgarly flaunt her rank and socially destroy those she considered inferiors.

"Must be terrible without civilization, all savages and wig-wams." Lady Ward's ostrich feathers fanned a breeze over Anthony's heated face.

Rachel cranked her neck to peer at the towering mass of Lady Ward's hair that dwarfed her husband by two feet. "We ill-bred Colonials have a saying that a donkey looks into the mirror and wonders at the charm of her own reflection."

Lady Ward inhaled, her ostrich feathers trembling.

Anthony smirked. The Yank could take care of herself.

The Duke of Banfield stomped his cane unable to contain his chortle. Lady Ward glared at him then pivoted her attention to Anthony. "How are your experiments?"

Rachel's lips took on a mutinous tilt. "Lord Anthony is soon to unveil something so spectacular it will set the world on end."

Lord Ward took a pinch of snuff. "You are young, Miss Thorne. How tragic."

"Are you sure a flower pot did not fall on your head?" Anthony scowled. The falling urn incident at the Chelmsford lay fresh in his mind.

Lord Ward narrowed his eyes. "So glad the pot missed you, Lord Anthony. Of this I am most sincere."

Anthony took a step toward Lord Ward. "I have learned a little sincerity is a dangerous thing. A great deal of it is absolutely fatal."

"Ah. Well. We must not monopolize your time." They bowed and drew back. "Magnificent ball."

Lord Banfield laid a detaining hand on Anthony's shoulder. "Cowards make the best bullies. They understand fear and know how to use it. Don't waste your time."

Anthony saw the worry that darkened Rachel's expression. His hands remained fisted.

"Both were so smug, but do you think Lord Ward might have been the one who tried to kill us with the flowerpot? Do you think he killed your lab assistant?" she asked.

"I have the same concerns. Lord Ward has the money, the influence, and the motive. He is a strong opponent to my father's policy in the House of Lords to end the costly war in the Colonies."

Rachel sighed. "I've made a mess of things tonight. I fell for Sir Bonneville's ruse to lure me to the library, and then I was far too outspoken with Lady Ward."

With an I-told-you-so look about the loathsomeness of balls, Anthony parroted her earlier remark. "To be nourished with new actions, new aspirations, new events will lend us new visions, won't it, Miss Thorne?" His broadside earned a pained expression from her.

Humphrey snorted. "Don't mind Lady Ward. She has nothing to offer the world except a headache, existing to parade her own equation between status and human worth."

"If anything, the evening is entertaining. Say whatever you like, Miss Thorne, I'll back you up completely," said the Duke of Banfield.

Rachel laid a hand on her heart. "I had no idea that there could be a creature as condescending as Lady Ward."

Difficult to tamp down the devil in him, Anthony said, "Lady Ward is not at fault."

Rachel groaned. "Which makes my comment all the worse."

Anthony observed the pasted tower of Lady Ward's hair bobbing and weaving through the crowd, a cat whiskers-width away from a candelabra. How many minutes for the confection to blaze from the start of ignition to her scalp? "As a cure-all, Lord Ward shocked her. A curiosity she's not a smoking crater on the carpet."

Rachel smiled and her happiness caused an unfamiliar lightness in him. *Risky.* Dangerous to fall under Rachel's spell. He began to move away, but she tugged his arm and raised her feathered brow in an aren't-you-going-to-ask-me-to-dance question.

"I don't know how to dance."

"I doubt that. Sir Jameson was ready to ask me again, and he can sneeze with enough force to put the planets out of alignment."

"He asked you to dance. Twice."

"Does that bother you?"

He pulled her onto the dance floor. "How diverting, the odds of being struck by lightning opposed to the odds of being killed by lightning."

Rachel pealed with hilarity, her laughter was like the first ray of light of God's creation. "For someone who cannot dance, you surprise me, Lord Anthony, with your fluidity."

"You do not think a duke's son would have refinements?"

She lifted her eyelashes. "Admit it, you are having fun, and if you wish to have more enjoyment, I can explain the science of what people are now thinking."

"Go ahead and divine your prophetic wanderings of the human mind. There's Lady Ward, tell me what she is thinking."

"That's easy. She is ready to roast me on spit."

"Wrong. She doesn't think. There is nothing there to think with."

Rachel giggled. "Her hair, to think it would make a perfect target for an archer's arrow."

"Don't tell me archery is another of your talents?"

"Living with savages and wigwams, one must be prepared. My brother, Ethan, taught me." She gave Anthony a shy smile, and then angled her head to the sidelines.

"Look at that man in the orange frockcoat. He's staring off in the distance, dreaming of a long lost lover."

"He's dreaming how he can escape his nagging wife and go fishing."

"That is unfair. You have a history of people that I don't have."

Her radiant smile made the millwheel spin. The evening had not been a waste of time and Anthony pondered that notion, for everything he did in life was arranged to eradicate randomness and remove chance. Control was his expertise—anticipating every possibility, foreseeing every response, and molding reality toward the desired outcome. With Miss Thorne, his world was turned upside down and dropped on its head.

Friends? Brother, she had called him. For the first time in his life he was unable to handle that disconnect. *Platonic? How tragic.* Plato would have an opinion. How about friends delving into a base and carnal nature?

"I suppose you can tell me what I'm thinking." *He hoped not.*

"Absolutely."

"Amazing because I don't even know my mind."

"You are thinking about getting back to your laboratory. Look over my shoulder, the man conversing with Lord Banfield…the man with the glass eye. He sends shivers down my spine. He is malevolent. He has a secret. There is anger."

Anthony snorted. "That is my Uncle Cornelius, Duke of Westbrook. He's been looking like that ever since your cousin, Captain Thorne captured his ships. Almost bankrupted him."

Anthony escorted her off the dance floor and Rachel unconsciously leaned into him. He liked her bending into him. "Don't worry, he's harmless."

"You are the student tonight," she reminded him. "Now tell me what I'm thinking."

He looked her up and down. Beneath soft brows were eyes a mystifying violet and he imagined, when her moods changed, were endless shades of lavender and blue lilac. "I haven't a clue."

Rachel waved her hand over the broodmare competition. "All this and I'll never marry."

"Why not?"

Her fingers twisted in his, and he barely caught her muttered words before someone took her for another dance.

"Because I'm not desirable."

Chapter 6

asping, Rachel sat up like a shot, her arms crossed protectively over her chest. Would she ever be able to eradicate the nightmares and terrors that haunted her? Abby had been her one true confidante, allowing into the darkness that swallowed Rachel, a glimmering of light. But Abby was an ocean away and she dared not confide her shame to anyone. She did not want what happened to her in Boston, and the humiliation of everyone treating her like an oddity to follow her to England.

The heavy gold drapes were peeled back and the sunshine spilled over her bed, warming her skin. Blinking against the brightness of the morning, she became aware of busy, rustling noises coming from inside her room.

"Good morning, Miss Thorne. I didn't mean to startle you, but you did tell me to wake you for breakfast," said Mrs. Noot, her assigned lady's maid, a middle-aged woman with curly brown hair tucked under her cap, her uniform, neat and crisp, denoting efficiency, yet severe in comparison to her lively and smiling manner.

Rachel fell back into the pillows, trying to slow her breaths, grateful for the brilliant day that chased away the gloom. She clutched and unclutched the gold damask coverlet, forcing the rich smoothness to ease her tremors. No doubt, Sir Bonneville's provocation triggered the nightmare. Although, she'd put on a strong façade, in truth, she had been terrified, panicking, her limbs useless to move. Thank God, Anthony had rescued her when he did.

A housemaid dusted the marble hearth, and then stoked smoldering embers. A fire flared to life in a gigantic fireplace. Rachel stared at the motifs of roses and cherubs on the ceiling, her sight descending to the walls painted a robin-egg blue and a darker hue of equivalent shades in rich velvet drapes that were secured with gold tassels. Her vanity was skirted with a harmonizing color and a blue brocade stool to match. Across the elegant room and housing a portion of her new gowns stood a massive walnut armoire with inlaid mother of pearl. The housemaid gathered her canvas and copper pot filled with the night's ashes and left.

"You have nothing to fear, Miss Thorne. You are safe in the Duke's house." Soft brown eyes gentled as did the grooves in her cheeks, lending a motherly appearance to Mrs. Noot.

Had she said something in her sleep?

Servants gossiped.

Rachel threw back the covers and planted her feet on the silky-smooth Aubusson rug of pink and sea foam green while Mrs. Noot laid out silk stockings and lacy underthings.

"I cannot possibly wear this gown." Rachel smoothed her hand over the silver brocade trimmed with silver bobbin lace along the hem, sleeves and bodice. If she spilled something on it in the lab, the gown would be destroyed. Neither could she tell Mrs. Noot she was working alone with Anthony. "I need something more serviceable, less weight, less cumbersome, less expansive…without the panniers. I wish to take a walk today."

Mrs. Noot produced a simple green linen gown that the seamstress had insisted on, making several for Rachel, informing her the new style was scandalously started by Queen Marie Antoinette in France. The chemise a la reine was incredibly light and simple, consisting of layers of thin muslin with a low-laced bodice, belted around the waist with a sash, fitted sleeves from shoulder to wrist and no panniers. Perfect for Rachel's work in the laboratory.

After helping Rachel dress, Mrs. Noot guided her to the vanity to do her hair. Gone was the chatty, effervescent, and welcoming maid. In the mirror's reflection, Mrs. Noot opened her mouth, and then snapped it shut. Was she on the brink of telling Rachel what she heard? Was she condemning her for an assault that was entirely out of Rachel's hands?

"Out with it," Rachel demanded. "What did I say in my sleep?"

Mrs. Noot moved across the room. "I can't seem to find the hairpins."

From her vanity, Rachel held up the crystal bottle of hairpins Mrs. Noot thought she had misplaced.

"I'm so happy you found them, Miss Thorne." She picked up a silver brush and started on Rachel's hair.

"You are avoiding my question."

Mrs. Noot stopped, brush midair. "I feel your pain, Miss Thorne…it happened to me."

Rachel felt the blood drain from her face. To hear the tragedy spoken aloud was even worse.

Mrs. Noot put her trembling hand on Rachel's shoulder. "I will keep your secret in the strictest confidence, my lady."

Rachel swallowed a hard lump.

Mrs. Noot set the brush on the vanity. "I will share my painful story, and I believe it will help. My husband, Cuthbert, was the Duke's former manager. How Cuthbert swept me off my feet. I considered myself lucky to be married to such a nice man. Under that layer of kindness was great cruelty. He took pleasure in humiliating, beating and raping me. Cuthbert was merciless with the Duke's tenants, but they were too afraid to go up against him. I stood up to him one day, told him I was going to report him to Duke Rutland. If Lord Anthony hadn't happened by... heard my screams..." She shook her head. "Anthony thrashed my husband. I had never known this side of Lord Anthony, always thought of him as a quiet scholar without a hint of violence. He became my young knight in shining armor. I am indebted to him for saving my life."

Mrs. Noot took a deep breath. "Cuthbert was dismissed and banished from the estate, yet that day is branded on my memory. I lost the child I was carrying, and almost died from hemorrhaging. Lady Lucretia, Lord Anthony's mother ordered me brought to the house to convalesce. When her lady's maid retired, I became her replacement."

Rachel clasped her maid's hand. Their eyes caught in the mirror, an unspoken acknowledgement that they belonged to a special club...thin fragile strings wound the shame and emotional vulnerability of two women into a thick cord that bound them.

"You said, was—"

"My husband is deceased. When Lady Rutland hired me on the heels of Cuthbert's dismissal, he flew into a jealous rage, burning down half of the Duke's stables in retribution. Prosecuted and sent to prison, he picked fights, his anger earning him an early death."

In a soothing tone, Mrs. Noot said, "To hold it in, Miss Thorne, is to freeze the pain. Know that I am here for you."

Rachel sat there for a long time, allowing the older woman to fuss over her hair, her lady-maid's way of offering compassion and mothering. Rachel's heart melted.

"You are ready, Miss Thorne."

Rachel rose and hugged her. "Thank you."

"Off you go, my lady," said a flustered Mrs. Noot.

Rachel descended the cantilevered stairs, the rich red carpet hushing her footsteps. She stopped midlevel and gazed out a huge leaded window that overlooked the vast estate of Belvoir Castle, catching the rising sun to best advantage. Beautiful Baroque gardens, dormant now, terraces, lawns, and a sleeping fountain of cherubs, announced gaiety to the world. There was so much to discover and explore.

The Rutland's ancestral home was just short of a palace. When Rachel had first clapped eyes on the magical structure she was beyond words. The façade dominated the landscape, stretching left to right of bulging, stonework, lending the building an air of unyielding authority, further accentuated by a powerful repetition of windows and turrets. The effect was dramatic. By no accident had Anthony's ancestors built the edifice on high ground so that anyone in the valley had to look uphill, almost compelling them to genuflect.

Her heels tapped a quiet tattoo across polished, opalescent marble floors to the dining hall, another room of rich splendor, accentuating red velvet walls and gold trim. A crystal chandelier, the length of a carriage painted rainbows on the opposing wall from the brilliant morning sun shining through the windows. Would she ever get used to the opulence? A footman seated her next to Anthony.

Coming from Boston, Rachel was used to rising early and she was glad that the Duke and Anthony were not disposed to the indolent lifestyle of their peers.

The Duke sat at the head of the table looking over *Lloyd's List* and the *London Gazette*. She couldn't get over how father and son radiated waves of regal authority, a trait she presumed, bred from birth, happenstance and experience.

The Duke probed a portion of kidney pie on his plate. "You enjoyed the ball last night."

It was a statement not a question. "I did, Your Grace."

"I understand, Miss Thorne, that Lady Ward was less than...I want to apologize for some of my countrymen."

Rachel blanched, then looked away. How much had he heard? Anthony shook his head. Not from him.

"Lady Ward and I had a misunderstanding—" Rachel made an extensive study of the eggs offered from the sideboard. Had he heard how she compared Lady Ward to a donkey? Would the duke send her packing back to Boston? Rachel buttered her croissant with the intense diligence Michelangelo sculpted the *Pieta*.

The duke lifted an eyebrow. "Your comparison to a particular equine was appropriate. I could not have phrased it better."

Rachel choked. But, was that a grin that the normally stoic butler was quick to conceal? She tried to remember his name. Sebastian? He stood next to the door, tall, beak-nosed, silver hair and grey eyes beneath beetle brows that discerned the air around him. He was lean and thoughtful, chest out, shoulders back and he gave the impression if he broke his posture, not only would it be an effrontery to himself but to humankind.

The Duke delved into a plate of bacon, enough to feed a whole army and selected the crispiest piece. "Too bad about Sir Bonneville. Broke his knee. Fell drunk, I suppose. Rather clumsy of him, don't you think, Anthony?"

Was there anything the Duke did not know?

A servant tonged three quail eggs to Anthony's plate, three clicks on bone china. He leaned back in his chair, and then winked at Rachel as though they were conspirators. "Bonneville, Lord and Lady Ward, all sail the same ship. What life has taught me is to never argue with idiots. They will grind you down to their level and beat you with experience."

Rachel was not used to the cloaked nuances of the Duke and Anthony. She was an American and Americans came out and said what they thought. She popped a cream puff in her mouth and closed her eyes. Had she gone to heaven? A servant filled her rose-patterned teacup from a silver gleaming teapot.

"Sugar? Cream?" He solicitously gestured to the foamy fresh cream and lumps of cubed sugar. The dressmaker would have to let out the waists on her gowns.

The Duke of Rutland put down his teacup. "Anthony, did I mention that Lady March has departed and your great Aunt Margaret is coming to visit? She loves your scientific mind and insists on sitting in your lab—all day."

Anthony slapped his hands on the arms of his chair. "Impossible. She is the farthest away from any scientific thinking. Never has she set one foot in my lab and never will she. I cannot have the interruption. I must concentrate and cannot afford to babysit Aunt Margaret."

The Duke cut his smoked salmon in three even pieces, put his knife and fork down, and then looked at his son, his meaning well-communicated. "She would like to meet *Miss Thorne*."

This time Rachel understood the doublespeak. To slither beneath the Persian rug had appeal. The Duke *knew* they had been working alone in the laboratory. He was protecting Rachel's reputation by making a chaperone available. He was thinking of her.

Anthony protested. "Aunt Margaret has fits of narcolepsy and snores loudly. Very loudly. She doesn't even know what planet she is on half the time."

The duke smiled. End of discussion. "Perhaps Aunt Margaret can work on your attire."

Anthony's blue eyes blazed. "What is wrong with my attire?"

"You have a predilection to be dressed for the day, cravat white, suit impeccable, yet two straight hours in your laboratory, you look like you've been through two wars. And get a shave."

Anthony rubbed the dark stubble on his handsome chin. "No time."

"It's a mandate, not a request."

With the preciseness of a Japanese samurai, Anthony cracked his quail egg. "I'll get it taken care of."

Before two volcanoes erupted, Rachel intervened. "I was thinking of the Parthian Battery."

Anthony tilted his dark head considering, then whipped out his notebook from his coat pocket. "The prehistoric battery using a clay jar that holds an iron rod surrounded by a copper cylinder and then filled with vinegar?"

The Duke interrupted. "About your shaving—"

"What of it?"

His father scowled. "I want it done daily."

"I'm not talking of shaving. I am responding to Miss Thorne. It is not effective for the type of battery we seek...produces little current."

Like keeping two badgers apart. She tried again although how much of a deterrent she would be, before father and son ended in a major verbal dispute would be a miracle. "The Babylonians employed a galvanic technique, using grape juice to apply gold plate to stoneware."

Anthony let out a loud breath. His hair tumbled down his forehead and she had the urge to sweep it up with her fingers. "I do not want gold plated stoneware."

Oh, the man was so stubborn. Couldn't he see what she was proposing? Rachel tilted her head back and skewered him with her eyes. "That is not my point. You use saltwater. Perhaps we need to try other solutions to harness a charge like the Babylonians accomplished, using grape juice."

"Not possible." Anthony rose and pulled out her chair.

"Do you ever allow your valet to shave you?" The duke's words were articulated in a short strong sentence but seemed so far away.

At this moment, she was bursting with ideas and needed to see them through. *Now.*

Rachel placed her hands on her hips. "And why not? There must be something else we haven't explored. You have already linked a set of glass-coated capacitors with metal deposited on each surface. Those capacitors were charged with a static generator and discharged by touching metal to their electrode, giving a stronger discharge. I've been thinking about making different electrochemical cells?"

"I have been thinking of using different metals."

"Now the wheels are turning. Like what?"

"Maybe zinc and iron?"

"Interesting. What is your theory?" Rachel nearly swooned thinking of the possibilities, Anthony grabbed her wrist and refused to let go, hurrying her out the doors.

The Duke called after them. "The sun is going to fall into the ocean tomorrow." The footman closed the doors and the duke nodded for everyone to leave except for his head butler.

"They never heard a word I said, did they, Sebastian?"

His head butler cleared his throat. "It does not appear so, Your Grace."

The duke drummed his fingers on the table. "What do you think?"

The butler harrumphed in condescension.

"So that's your opinion."

The butler poured the Duke another cup of tea. "It is not my place to say, Your Grace."

The Duke smiled. "It is exactly what Abby has orchestrated. I'd say she's right."

Sebastian's tone was brisk. "And how is that, Your Grace?"

The Duke came right to the point. "A match made in heaven. To get Anthony out of his isolation. Miss Thorne is worth her weight in gold."

The butler lifted his chin with dawning realization. "I see your point, Your Grace. Perfect."

Lord Rutland shook out his newspaper to read. "You old fox, you came to that conclusion before I did."

The butler smiled.

Chapter 7

*O*n the way to the laboratory, Rachel threaded her hand through Anthony's arm, a most natural thing to do, since she was accustomed to doing the same with her brother and cousin. To the east, the bright light of morning consumed the rising mists.

"I demand a quid pro quo today in payment for my services," she teased. He lost a step, recovered, and then nodded to one of the guards posted, making her mindful of the danger that followed the Rutland family.

"An equal exchange of what?"

A rabbit scurried through the naked branches of a rose bush, startling a coaltit to flight. Rachel jumped and gripped Anthony's arm. Beneath the stiffness of his coat, she felt his strong muscles flex and wondered how a man with Anthony's propensity to work indoors could be so muscular.

He opened the door to the laboratory, allowing her to enter first. A fire blazed in the fireplace, and she moved toward the warmth, evaporating the outside chill.

Though devoid of anyone else, a strange and dynamic presence lingered in every corner of the masculine laboratory. Rachel smelled it in the pungent scents of chemicals, and beeswax rubbed into the cherry cabinets and massive desk.

"I would like to go on a tour of the estate," she said over her shoulder. Before he had a chance to dig in his heels, she pivoted on him, the rustling of her skirts disturbing the peaceful purity of the stillness. "It's only fair. Besides the fresh air will do us good."

He grumbled something about conspiracies to distract him, and then contracting pneumonia. She laughed, moving past the counters stocked with bottles and equipment to retrieve one of Anthony's aprons draped on a hook, looped it around her neck and tied it in the back to protect her gown.

"What should we work on first?"

"I could launch a litany of scientific responses, but defer to you, Miss Thorne. You are so full of shining ideas and idealism. We will try your concept of changing the chemical solution."

Anthony shrugged out of his frockcoat, tossed it on a stool then rolled up his sleeves. His forearms bulged, muscled and strong like a blacksmith who spent his day lifting a heavy hammer and pounding iron. This confirmed what she had felt beneath her fingers.

Why was she suddenly nervous being alone with him? Was it the intimacy that the lab allowed? Preying on her conscience was what she had almost revealed—something very private to him the night before. Fortunately, the noise level at the ball hid her impulsive burst. For Anthony to raise questions on why she was undesirable would be too humiliating and the last thing she wanted was for him to think of her as a social pariah like the men in Boston had.

He withdrew to the window. "I miss my sister. She was always in my lab, sat on that chair and watched me do my experiments. One night changed everything in our lives."

She moved beside him. "I try to put myself in Abby's shoes, waking up in the dark bowels of a ship. The horrors she faced aboard the *Civis* under a former slaver captain bent on her demise. So fortunate Jacob captured the merchantman when he did. Abby's resourcefulness was amazing, disguising herself as a boy. I can imagine the chagrin on my proud cousin's face when he discovered a female on board his ship."

She smiled up to him. "How fortunate everything worked out in the end. They had a lovely wedding ceremony and now the treasure of a beautiful baby boy. They are so happy."

Anthony leveled her a droll look. "If anyone had told me two years ago that my sister would be married to a notorious privateer, I would have said they were crazy."

She rubbed her forearms. "Even though Abby was safe in Boston with Jacob, there was one person I feared afterward that might have caused Abby and your family trouble, and that was Captain Davenport."

Anthony smirked. "Captain Davenport's hubris earned him a promotion to India for an indefinite stay. That my father had any influence with his cousin, the King, I can only guess."

"That will teach me not to fool with a Rutland." Rachel cleared her throat and moved the balance scale to where they were working. "I spoke with Mrs. Noot, my lady's maid. She told me how you saved her from her husband."

"If there was ever a piece of humanity that symbolized cruelty, it was Cuthbert. He beat his wife like a rented mule."

"You impressed Mrs. Cuthbert with your...talents?"

Anthony swiveled to face her. "Miss Thorne, you are provocative."

Elbows resting on the counter, Rachel rested her chin in the palm of her hand. "It's just that—"

"Like Mrs. Noot, you expected me to be soft since I closet myself in my laboratory? I box regularly with tenants. They work hard to keep me in good shape."

"Oh, dear, I hope you didn't think I was being indelicate." She twirled hair around her finger and then caught him staring at the movement, stopped and straightened, running her hands down her apron front.

"Not at all. I like your curious nature. I encourage it."

Never had she felt so alive. To whirl around with her arms outstretched.

"You never completed telling me of your archery exploits."

Rachel bit her lip. "You can thank Reverend Pott's wife for my archery abilities."

"Was she your tutor?"

"She was my inspiration. Mrs. Potts had a predilection for gossip and meanness. She was also afraid of Indians, even though the few that were around lived in remote areas outside of Boston or, like the friendly Wampanoag, worked on ships and farms. But you couldn't convince Mrs. Potts of their civilized ways. When she started terrible rumors about Jacob, Ethan and me, we went on the offensive. We made a huge supply of arrows, and then went out into the forest to practice with our bows, competing with each other."

"I see where this is going."

He looked like summertime, if one could look like a favorable season, warm and thriving.

Forcing down a smile, Rachel let loose her story. "First, I launched an arrow next to her front door. She nearly fainted dead away. Every day I launched more arrows, her back door, bedroom window, her carriage. When she had said something particularly mean-spirited about my younger brother, Thomas who was all of two summers, and the dearest, sweetest little boy who walked the earth, I ramped up the bombardment that would have made Julius Caesar proud. I loved Thomas and for Mrs. Potts to call him such awful names was abominable. Every time she went to the privy, she came under attack. I launched a dozen arrows into the door. Mrs. Potts swooned, and did not leave the privy all day, fearing Indians had invaded Boston. My father caught me and I received quite a penance."

"What was your penance?"

"I could not go to the shipyard for a whole day. My father did not like Mrs. Potts either, but he had to make a point."

"No doubt the rebellious streak runs in the family. I'll have to be on my best behavior lest you come after me with your bow and arrows."

Rachel laughed. Anthony referred to her older brother and cousin, staunch rebel privateers against the Crown with a price on their heads.

"I have failed." She sighed.

"Failed? How's that?"

"My goal was to turn your perpetual scowl into a cheerful countenance."

"An impossible feat."

"And why is that?" She wanted to know the dark mysterious side of Anthony Rutland. The part that held him back from living.

She bit her lip. Were they not both full of flaws, stitched together with good intentions and seeking...seeking what? She could not answer that question for the life of her.

Not wanting to let the gaiety of the moment subside, she asked, "It's only fair you share with me one of your youthful foibles."

Anthony exhaled, obviously weighing what he would reveal to her. "When I was twelve summers, I experimented with different chemicals, left the combinations heating over the fire, and then left for lunch. My absence precipitated an explosion."

"You mean to tell me your laboratory has suffered two explosions?"

Anthony nodded. His hair was a mess, loosened from his queue and there was a stain on his upper sleeve. At that moment, he was the handsomest man in the world.

He fidgeted with several flasks, probing his creative mind. "If we spilt the making of the solutions then we will be more efficient."

She moved to the counter and drew out some flasks, and then reached for the sulfuric acid on the shelf above. The bottle wobbled, tilted, her fingers grasping. The carafe spun from her reach, and then dropped. A scream squelched in her throat. Her heart stopped. A wind brushed against her. Anthony swooped up and caught the bottle. The stopper popped out and rolled across the counter, the oily residue, steaming a path where acid burned the work surface. Had the acid splashed on her hands? She stared with horror, waiting for the fire of the acerbic to blister her skin.

He set the bottle down, grabbed her, and dragged her to a sink. With violence, he worked the pump, water flushing out the spout and onto her hands. Repeatedly, he inspected her skin through a cascade of water. A jolt ran through her from his unexpected touch.

She shook her head. "I don't think the acid splashed on my skin."

His eyes narrowed on her…eyes that masked the soul and in the same instant, snapped and crackled points of fire. Was he one of those men who didn't want you to think they were interested in you, even though they were? "Acid eats flesh, devours bone." He reprimanded her—but she knew that.

How stupid.

"You will be more careful," he commanded. "I am responsible for you and don't want to see you get hurt."

Rachel pulled her hands away, surprised that her shaking limbs obeyed her. Her careless handling of the acid made her want to slither under the door like a snake to escape. And if her inept actions weren't embarrassing enough, she'd obviously read far more into his responses than existed. He was gallant and concerned for her safety. What a fool to assume he cared for her more than a colleague.

He yanked open a drawer and jerked on rubber gloves. "We will not perform the acid test today. We will explore what I have in mind. The Italian physician, Galvani used iron and brass in his experimentation. I'm thinking he was on to something in utilizing two dissimilar metals." He scrubbed the counter and put the sulfuric acid bottle on the shelf.

Her stomach clenched at his easy dismissal of her theory, as if her concept had no merit at all. "We will revisit my theory in the future?" By no means was she going to allow her idea to be swept away.

"Most people are superstitious about electricity, believing this fire we produce is divined from the devil."

Was he intimating that the acid disaster was bad luck? He tore off his gloves and tossed them aside. "We will continue using the saltwater solution."

Pig-headed man. "We need to try an acid."

"I hate eating Lord Ward's dust."

She planted her fists on her hips. "Then listen to my theory."

"I will, but I want to rule out the salt-water. My suspicions are nagging me. Can you mix a brine, thirty percent salt, sixty percent water? I'll retrieve the zinc and iron plates."

Your laboratory, Lord Anthony.

Rachel lowered her head, measuring out the salt and water and mixing the solution. Abby had told her that Anthony had been married. To have snared the highly intelligent, talented Lord Rutland, the woman must have been clever...and beautiful. Good Lord, was she jealous of a dead woman?

He brushed against her and her head snapped up. For a split second she sensed he had the urge to touch her again, and yet, in his eyes, shuttered a flash of pain. He pulled back. What demons tormented him? Did the ache he buried have something to do with his late wife?

How had his wife dealt with his flaws? Judgmental? Impatient? Sometimes rude? The strong opinions he formed? But, in a room full of people, hadn't he challenged Lord Ward, making threats and insults that would curl one's ears? Hadn't he subdued Sir Bonneville? As brash as Americans were considered, Lord Anthony outdistanced them in crossing the lines of respectable boundaries. The man was an enigma.

What others might find pushy or callous, Rachel viewed through a different lens. She saw and respected the intelligent and gifted man who held himself to the highest of standards. She laughed off his brooding insults and accepted his impatience as a positive virtue.

It was all a façade. With her, he was kind, considerate and honorable. That he adhered to a code of ethics, regarding her was demonstrated when he saved her from Sir Bonneville and then again, when he had saved her life. She liked the way he cared for her. *Protected her.*

His analytical mind drove her wild and his drive to succeed matched her desire to excel. He was a man with a vision and a man to get things done. With discovery a food for his soul, and the ability to conquer the world, nothing would stop him.

He procured the items he needed and then threw extra logs on the fire. Sparks spit and snapped and spiraled up the flue. "Experimentation is more forceful than any logical thinking: facts can destroy our reasoned train of thought—not the other way around," he said.

He referred to Dr. Galvani's experimentation in making frog's legs jump, deeming living tissue yielded electricity. Anthony believed otherwise. He rejoined her, the firelight dancing off the broad angles of his face as he focused on placing the plates side by side.

She nodded her head in agreement. "And the day scientists study non-physical phenomena will be the day man advances with enormous strides."

He leaned into her. Rachel stepped back. Of course, he would be doubted, disagreed with, and disapproved, going up against a tsunami of naysayers in the scientific community for his theories. Her heart ached. His journey would be difficult.

He stared at her. "Thank you for your confidence in me."

The air in the laboratory was suddenly too close. Too thick and full and overflowing with——him. Determined not to let her guard down Rachel raised her chin and did her best to look him square in the eye.

She numbered the many startling contrasts of Lord Anthony, adding up to a complex mix of confidence, idealism and stubborn persistence. A pang of longing shot through her.

To be with such a man.

Invisible chains dragged her down...she couldn't yoke Anthony with her shame. She couldn't allow herself to fall in love with him because she would drag him down and ruin his brilliant career.

His jaw flexed. "I think by alternating the zinc and iron we will have some success in storing energy. Let's try more plates. Can you get me more from the cabinet?" She fixed her gaze on the cabinet at the side of the room, hiding her discomfiture behind a carefully arranged mask of serenity.

Before the near rape, she had been the delight of Boston. No longer. When she recovered people treated her different. Men stared, women whispered gossip. With her parents dead and her brother and cousin off privateering, she had been alone, facing a cruel world. Good men, who had shown interest before, now made excuses. Even though she'd done nothing wrong, she'd felt like a pariah, and her heart ached at the unfairness.

Agnes Quick, a wealthy widow and neighbor had seen the problem for what it was and had made it her mission to put Rachel back on the map. Afterwards, the ladies of Boston became more generous and invited her to social events. Yet, the desirable men were still put off. The invisible social barrier remained steadfast.

Not once did Anthony take his eyes off her sojourn to the cabinet and back. She moistened her lips as she handed him the discs. His hand glided across hers, warm and confident, as he accepted them from her.

She took a deep breath. "Hydraulics and electricity are similar sciences. I believe all energy flows along a path," she said, putting every bit of crisp, Yankee efficiency she'd gained over the years into her voice, quieting the tremors.

He lifted a brow. "Yes, I know."

She blinked. Anthony's calm calculation had returned. Had what she'd seen been a trick of the firelight? He finished the disc arrangement, inserted the assembly in a bowl.

She poured the salt solution over the discs. "How did Duke Cornelius come to possess a glass eye? An injury, or an anomaly at birth?" She picked up a quill, dabbed it in the inkbottle, and recorded notes on their progress.

"Lost his eye in a sword fight."

She breathed in Anthony's scent, chemicals and sandalwood. He wrinkled his forehead, engrossed with his task and did not notice how close they were working together. She rather liked his warmth and nearness. But they were friends, working toward a goal. No need to muck it up with romantic inclinations.

"He was in a swordfight with my father, a fight over my mother."

Rachel's head snapped up, her pen creating a loud scratch against the table. "That is an interesting anecdote."

"My mother married my father and all was forgiven years later."

Rachel did not possess the same feeling of the tall, dark-featured, Duke Cornelius. He may have made amends, been a close family friend, but he reminded her of a giant shark her brother had caught...the same cold black unblinking eye and, for a moment, she imagined gill slits on the side of his head.

"We are ready for the test."

Rachel held her breath and prayed it would work.

He stuck a wire to the ends of the discs. A small charge flared and faded away, vanishing into nothingness. "Damn." He raked his fingers through his hair and turned away. "I will never succeed."

Rachel sagged, watching him pace back and forth. "Don't give up."

"The charge is not enough."

"Allow the million little defeats to be the rungs on a ladder, each one that you climb to success. Persistence and patience will stand the hallmark of your triumph."

The door shoved open. Rachel swung around to see a visitor.

Anthony's voice came low, as if he were growling. "Aunt Margaret."

A servant escorted a petite, plump, grey-haired woman to a chair while another deposited a tray on a side table. An animal horn lay drooped on the older woman's chest.

"Time for tea, Anthony. Come here, dear boy and introduce me to the lovely Miss Thorne who I have heard so much about from Abby's letters."

Anthony gave his matronly aunt a kiss on the cheek, made introductions, and then pulled up two stools, one for Rachel and one for himself. A crude seating arrangement, but charming none the same while a servant poured tea, and then departed. It was afternoon and the culinary delights made Rachel's stomach rumble. *Creampuffs*. She tonged two of the flaky pastries onto her plate and a small flan. Her mouth puckered with the sweet-sour of a gooseberry tart. She let out a moan.

"It is so nice to meet you," Rachel said.

Aunt Margaret reared back horrified. "I would never beat you."

Anthony looked to Rachel. "Let me try. My hair is on fire."

Aunt Margaret smiled and nodded. "Okay, in a while."

Rachel dabbed a napkin over her mouth to hide her lips. "Shame on you, Anthony. I like your Aunt Margaret. She is sweetness."

"I am so glad you came and agreed to be my chaperone," Rachel offered.

Aunt Margaret tsked and shook her head. "The King should never be overthrown. Such talk is treasonous."

"Oh, dear," Rachel said. "I've created a muddle."

Anthony gestured to the horn. Rachel had seen silver ear horns in the Colonies used for those who were hard of hearing. The funnel shaped device collected sound waves, amplified them and brought the communication to the ear.

Aunt Margaret held it to her ear, appearing like a half-Viking. "This is my new ear horn," she said proudly.

"What kind is it?" Rachel asked.

Aunt Margaret looked at the clock hanging on the wall. "A quarter after two."

Anthony slapped his hands on his knees. "Back to work." He escorted Rachel to their experiment in progress.

Rachel giggled. "Poor Aunt Margaret."

"Don't let her deafness fool you, and above all, do not fall prey to her innocent confusion that masks the nature of her genius. Except for frequent attacks of narcolepsy where the rest of the world ceases for her, she has a practiced eye for concealed disasters."

To prove his point, snoring and very loud snoring burst from behind. Aunt Margaret slumped in her chair, asleep. On impulse, Rachel went into the back room, tore a blanket off the cot and covered Aunt Margaret, careful to tuck in the covers around her.

"She is exhausted from her journey."

"They are preparing to leave, Your Grace, for an extended carriage ride," said Sebastian, the butler, closing the library doors behind him.

The duke strode to the window, the butler behind him watching the young couple. "The Colonial induced Anthony out of his lab. Can you imagine? Let's have a toast. An incredible accomplishment." The Duke of Rutland poured a glass of sherry for them both.

"Aren't you going to offer a drink to me?" A voice demanded behind a large wing-backed chair. "And shame on you for assuming the plot to keep them together is between the two of you."

The duke arrested his drink halfway—Aunt Margaret in the library?

Sebastian straightened, put his drink down and resumed his position. "If that is all you require, Your Grace, then I shall be on my way."

"Nonsense. Stay, Sebastian." Aunt Margaret waved a hand. "You two think you are the only ones privy to secrets. I wouldn't be left out of this for a million pounds. Abby wrote to me—" Their gazes locked as they assessed one another, confirming an unsaid secret, the duke taken aback by his wife's diminutive sister.

He threw back the entire contents of his glass, and then confirmed her accurate conclusion with a slight, mocking inclination of his head. "Well since we are all in the know, what do you suggest?"

Aunt Margaret blinked owl eyes, her superiority conveyed. "We must be clever for they are both very intelligent. I come from the days where a little distance makes the heart grow fonder. Let us think of something to separate them for a while."

The butler cleared his throat. "If I may speak, Your Grace, Lady Margaret's strategy has a purpose."

The duke nodded his head. "How do you propose that scenario when we can't tear them apart from that absurd electrical fire they swoon about?"

"Abby disclosed Miss Thorne was an inventor of sorts, had invented an indoor bathing tub, including a pump to move water upstairs. You could employ her to build one."

"And how would I do that? To retain her is the epitome of rudeness."

"Guilt and pride are powerful tools. Guilt is the bread and butter of many family communications."

"And pride?" the Duke prompted.

Aunt Margaret pursed her lips dubiously. "You're the expert."

She let that comment sit for a while. His lifelong assumptions on his wife's guileless sister vanished, and his opinion of Aunt Margaret climbed another notch.

"The girl takes great importance in her work. You need a bathtub and would appreciate her talents. Simple as that."

"I see," he said, but that infuriating quirk of her lips told him he'd just amused her.

"You better take charge and communicate your need as soon as possible." She looked like a goose ready to snap, rose, and the butler rushed to open the door, nodding his approval.

The duke raised a supercilious brow. "I see where all the cunning comes from in the family. You could box the ears of the best of the King's courtiers."

Aunt Margaret snorted. "It's taken you years to understand that? I congratulate you on your accomplishment and accept your acknowledgement as a compliment."

"It wasn't meant as a compliment. I despair and remain thankful you are on our side. If King George put you up against King Louis IVI, all of France would flee to Germany."

Anthony took Rachel's hand and helped her into the open carriage. They had worked for several hours while Aunt Margaret slumbered, and then escorted his aunt back to the house. If only to work in his lab longer to recover from another failed experiment.

But he'd promised Rachel a tour of the estate and was unable to refuse her.

How pretty she looked, wrapped in a black velvet cape bordered with ermine. "Lord Ward entertains all kinds of morbid amusements. His kind have no respect for science."

Anthony frowned at the guard following them, hating the idea that he was a prisoner in his home, but Rachel's blue eyes glowed like winter turning to a warm summer lit sea and her excitement was infectious, making him forget his jailer.

"We are not going to think about Lord Ward and let him spoil our outing," she commanded.

Anthony raised an eyebrow at her bold decree, climbed in beside her and laid thick furs across their laps. Harnessed in front, two matching black bays shook their manes and pawed the ground eager to be off. Anthony snapped his wrists and rippled the lines. The huge horses in perfect unison sprinted down the road and into the vast forests surrounding his ancestral home.

"Isn't it delightful to get out and get some fresh air? Enlivens the brain."

He couldn't have agreed more. *Nothing like glacial cold to tamp down the mounting fire in his body.* Hours of trying to concentrate on his work left him wanting, her intellect sweeping over him like a carnal caress. It was not logical. How could he control his body? There must be some sense made to this madness. He exhaled, the air forming a perfect cloud.

"I have accomplished the impossible and have pulled you from your laboratory."

Was there enchantment in her smile?

"If you like frostbite and the bitter cold, cutting you with a hundred knives."

Rachel giggled. "Acknowledge all the beauty before us. How the afternoon sun glitters off the snow-burdened branches and hills, and the slight wind that tosses the tops of the towering oaks and whistles softly through their lower limbs, its power diminished by the thickness of the forest. So silent and peaceful as if the forest is holding its breath."

"All I hear is the ringing in my ears where sound is frozen and the cracking of my iced-up face when I speak."

"That sound from your face cracking is a smile born. Admit it, you are enjoying yourself."

"I think you are eccentric," he huffed.

She leaned into him to speak conspiratorially, and he savored her warmth. "My eccentricity has taken years of dedicated effort to acquire."

"No doubt. What next, Miss Thorne, chattering with cold until my teeth break? Or something industrious that a Colonial privateer would do, hanging my frozen body from the yardarm until the crows have picked their fill?"

"You are hopeless."

He chose a less traveled road, and yielded to a cloying compulsion to detour toward what made Miss Thorne tick. *Why had she said she would never marry?* "This visit is about obtaining a husband?"

She stiffened beside him.

"You're the same age as Abby, two and twenty," he argued with his own smile of bemusement. "That's hardly in your dotage."

Because I'm not that desirable. His heart gave a kick. Couldn't get out of his head what she had muttered at the ball when she thought he hadn't heard. She then piqued his curiosity in the science of what people were thinking, needing to understand why someone of Rachel's loveliness would think she was not attractive?

"So why are you disinclined to the institution of marriage?"

She gave a snort of dismissive laughter. "Silly me. That was nothing."

She had passed the matter off too quickly. He was sensitive to her. Denial was an ordinary response to an atrocity, banishing the ability to feel. He should know, he repressed the feeling every day of his life. He'd not push her to tell him, but her voice reached out to him like the unexpected tendrils of a swirling galaxy, where she was involved and impacted by some dust and stars, but a lot of it was exogenous to her. He shrugged, perhaps a childhood trauma or something that happened to her during the war with the Colonies.

"I'd never dream of perpetuating such a tragedy. I have no wish to be any man's trouble, or wife."

So, she was disillusioned toward the idea of a husband. The road narrowed for a mile, and far below a raging river churned and eddied over sharp rocks.

"So dangerous. I'd hate to think of anyone falling off the road." She shuddered.

Clever how she changed the subject. He was sure there was more to her story. He had seen a glimpse of fear in her eyes when Bonneville had cornered her. How her manner contrasted to the natural way she took his hand and pulled him on the dance floor. The painting in the Rutland library came to mind. *The experiences of our past are the architects of our present.* What haunted Miss Thorne? What had happened in her past?

"What are you thinking of at the moment?" she asked.

He looked down at her rosy cheeks and full lips. "I'm thinking geometry." He didn't dare tell her the fundamental diagram of her face was the same as the one of the whole body; the link between the two, the height of the face is equal to the vertical distance between the middle of the body and intersection of the legs and the navel is equal to the distance between the tip of the middle finger. If he drew a line upward from the navel, he could measure two impressive spheres then estimate the height, weight and distance. And if he leaned in just a bit, his lips would meet hers...

Mesmerized by her rapt attention, he forced his gaze away. But, to be honest, the hell with all that geometry. He'd rather sample the spheres.

"It would give me insight if you told me what you were thinking."

To tell her what he was thinking, would show his depravity. Definitely show his depravity. Concentrate. Think. "What did you ask?"

Rachel sighed. It was an exasperated sigh but on her, it was how he imagined a sigh would sound after a long, lovely night of lovemaking. Except Rachel was an innocent. And he was inexperienced. Nonetheless his body reacted. Rock hard reacted.

"My father is pushing me into the role of duke which means my brother... He sighed. It means he is beginning to give up hope of finding Nicholas. I refuse to yield to that notion. Nicholas is out there. I feel it in my bones."

"The world is full of peril and there are many dark places, but we must always have hope."

Her wisdom although inspiring, gave way to an unfortunate reality. "I have no inclination to be the duke. To idle over tenant disputes, bookkeeping and accounting. Pure hell. Already my father has forced me into some of the duties. I was never made for that role. Detest it. Nicholas was made for the task. Science is my first and last mistress."

Her hood fell back and she tossed her chestnut curls. "I can understand your difficulty. After seeing a fraction of the estate, the duty is onerous. A mind like yours belongs in discovery."

Silence reigned. The soft, muted thud of the horse's hooves, the whisper of the carriage wheels over the snow and a woodpecker emerging from a hollow of a tree, a soft churr-churr invitation to its mate.

"I want to thank you for saving me from Sir Bonneville. I don't know what I would have done if you hadn't arrived in time." She shivered from the memory.

"I should have torn his right arm off and beat him with it."

Rachel pealed out her laughter and the sound rippled over the cedars and firs. He frowned. As a scientist, he was compelled to follow what was most probable, but in speculative thought, he was compelled to follow the fact that he liked to see her laugh.

"You discuss brawling like the price of potatoes," she said unable to control her mirth. "Oh, my, what is that?"

Anthony stopped the carriage, looking at the line of dormers set like a row of teeth in the third floor attic, visible now due to winter and the trees bare of their leaves. "That's Elijah Johnson's home, and old sea captain friend of my father's."

"Has he been at sea overlong? The disrepair—"

Anthony regarded the swayback sheds, and tumbled down and forsaken mansion. Surrounded by high oaks, branches extending horizontally, harshly angled, twisted, interlocked, grasping downward and upward, casting shadows of gloom and threatening anyone to enter.

"He died. His brother, a retired sea captain who lives in the town has not had the heart to tear the house down and this grand old dame has decayed into ruin."

"Sends chills up my spine..." she swayed into him. "...like someone is watching us."

He could not have agreed to a more hostile environment that left him uncharacteristically on edge.

He snapped the reins as they moved along the undulating road, to the town declining sharply southward in the valley, close-girdling the crescent mountain to the west. "He was an odd recluse, a hoarder, making up for the loneliness and guilt of losing his wife at sea. She had insisted on accompanying him on a voyage despite his rabid denial of the dangers. A terrible storm swept her overboard."

"What a sad tale."

"According to his brother, some rooms you could only sidestep through. He was numb with grief and sorrow, and wasted away."

Anthony knew that agony of living. He awoke each morning with the need to accomplish, to exist, as effortless as it appeared and as unmanageable as it truly was, contented. In the course of each day, his heart would drop from his chest into his belly. Before the sun left the day, he was overcome with nothingness, nothing but the desire to be alone, to be contented with the magnitude of his pointless guilt. To be alone in his loneliness? *I am not miserable.*

To convince himself of this had become an art. To convince others had become a masterpiece.

Rachel's lavender and lemon balm scent trailed over him, snaring him in its tentacles. He didn't believe the ray of sunshine that sat beside him was fooled for one second.

From the shadows of a cracked window, Cuthbert Noot clenched his fists watching a carriage withdraw from the sea captain's home he had commandeered since his escape.

"To the last, I will destroy Lord Anthony. From Hell's bowels, I will make him pay until I spit my last breath. Meant to kill him in his lab. Surprised his assistant. Couldn't keep a witness around," Cuthbert cackled.

Playing cards behind him, his brutal companions grunted.

Cuthbert had chosen well. The worst inhabitants of St. Giles, criminals from the Rookery underworld of London who found pleasure in slitting a man's throat for a farthing. The man named Scar the foulest among them.

"So many events to hate him for…my wife lives in splendor, as a lady's maid…would have died in prison if it wasn't' for that rich bloke. How good to kill Anthony's, wife. Easy to knock her off her horse. While she gasped for breath, I spread her milky white thighs and pounded my quid into her, savoring the screams of that whore of a wife of his…would have liked to extend my time, but that rich bloke got tired of watching…ordered me to break her neck to look like a fall from a horse. Crack. How easy to snap. That rich bastard didn't want any Rutland seed to flourish."

His companions laughed.

Cuthbert stroked his chin. "I see his lordship has an attachment to the Colonial? My quid throbs with a million things to do to her. Damn. Why do I have to follow that rich bloke's rules?"

Scar joined him at the window. "I'd like a turn with her. What the boss don't know, won't hurt him."

The rich bloke was a scary bastard and it took a lot for Cuthbert Noot to be scared of anyone. "I like playing games with Lord Anthony. Sent him a warning with the urn. Loved seein' his face when he found his dead assistant."

Cuthbert pressed his face against the glass to catch a final glimpse of the object of his hatred. "Feel safe with your Yank, Lord Anthony. Joy will turn to ashes in your mouth, and you'll know the debt is paid."

Chapter 8

*A*nthony raked his fingers through his hair. Weeks had melded into two months and nothing. Stimulants madly indulged his mind...electricity...and Rachel Thorne.

"Our errors are a result of simple bad luck." She placed glass tubes in a rack, running her fingers down their glistening length.

His mouth went dry. How erotic. What would she taste like? Cinnamon? Spice? Lemon? "I do not believe in luck. Everything I do is designed to eliminate randomness and eradicate chance. To deduce every possibility, predict every response, and mold experimentation toward a desired outcome."

"I want to know your thoughts on the Leyden jar." He watched her walk across the lab to retrieve another flask, her hips swung with the practiced ease of a courtesan, except she was no courtesan. She was tall, inches shorter than his six foot two frame with padding in all the right places, undeniably the right places.

Anthony said nothing. He was good at saying nothing. He could say nothing for the rest of his life and be content. He should waltz her out of his lab, lock the door and stay inside for the rest of his life. Yes, he could do it. And he could hurl the Thames River back to its source.

While Aunt Margaret snored in the corner, Rachel turned to him, with concentration. After a long silence elapsed, her brow furrowed, expectant of him to fill the void with what he was thinking.

Anthony scrubbed a hand over his jaw. Why he was no different than a useless dog, panting outside the butcher's shop?

"The Leyden jar has an alternating current that flows and bangs, pumping and thrusting, sliding and straining violently along a course." Had he just said that?

Thank the higher powers she was immersed in pouring a saline solution over the brass and nickel discs that she did not hear him.

Anthony held his breath and attached the wires. A small burst of electrical fire, and then nothing. He cursed beneath his breath.

Rachel knitted her brow in a way that gave Anthony the sense she was trying to figure out how best to say, *I told you so.*

"My miscalculations have brought a tempest of unforeseen challenges. We will use your sulfuric acid suggestion tomorrow."

She beamed her approval. Why did her happiness mean so much to him?

Aunt Margaret quit snoring, sat up and blinked at the clock. "Heavens, it is well past the time to leave, Miss Thorne."

Anthony scowled. "Where are you going? I cannot work without you."

"A ball followed by entertainment. Do you want to join us?" Rachel licked her lips with cautious hope.

"Absolutely not. The most illogical convention known to mankind."

"Sometimes it is good to be illogical," she chastised him. "Lady Imogene Brougham is going to sing. They say she is a sensation."

"Her singing presents the same sensation as barnacles scraped off the bottom of a ship, except the hull of the ship remains safe and sound. The damage to your ears is catastrophic."

"So you'll come?" Rachel reached up and smoothed his hair back, jolted him. He tamped down his reaction, told himself her touch was the same given to her brother.

She smiled then, the kind of smile that started the phase transition of ice to water to evaporation. All day long he had watched her as she moved about his lab, imagining the incredibly long legs under her skirts. Even the way she consumed those wretched cream puffs drove him mad, entering between her full lips, licking the cream from the side of her mouth with the right amount of seductiveness. It was best she left with Aunt Margaret to tea. At least he'd be able to breathe again.

When they were gone, he stared at the back of the door and a hushed void filled the laboratory. He sat in her vacated chair with nothing but silent air and the lavender and lemon scent from her body. Like long sharp needles, roots of loneliness crept through his insides. Anthony looked out the window, across the row of newly planted arborvitae and where a splattering of snow lay over a field of brown grasses. A frigid mist skirted the dark, grey woods. Ice covered gorse surrounded a lake's edge, adding to the surrealness of the landscape and all at once, a flash of memory assailed him...

"I'm going out riding." Celeste slapped her gloves across her hands with a youthful pout.

"Again? You are gone every day." She was so young, seventeen summers and had hounded him with her peach-colored skin and bright violet eyes, and hair, the red-gold of amber.

Celeste trilled. "My Lord, you are busy in your lab and will not miss me. Besides, I love to ride." She leaned up on her tiptoes and gave him a sisterly peck on the cheek. The only intimacy she allowed.

"Do you want me to go with you?"

She pursed her lips. "And take you away from your experiments? Wouldn't think of it."

Anthony shook his head sharply, straining to wipe away the unsettling memories. God, would it constantly be like this? Four long years had eclipsed, and still he was tormented by his inadequacy into looking after her, the past entombing him beneath a shadowy shroud.

Would he ever be free of Celeste? Would he have loved her if given more time? Was he capable of love? To experience a love like his mother and father who adored each other…a grab for the farthest reaches of the universe?

Hadn't Celeste pursued him, treating Anthony with golden deference and worshipping everything he said? Smiles and warm charm, she had everyone convinced of her value. His mother had died in childbirth and Celeste had charmed the Duke from his melancholies.

"A good match…you are well past the time to marry, Anthony…"

If only he'd not been driven by his father into the fatal words, *"I do."* To experience a new Celeste, remote and distant, faultfinding and disdaining while keeping up a public persona that said otherwise.

Independent of his father, Anthony had accrued a huge estate from his patents and investments. When Celeste discovered his assets, she spent huge amounts on her wardrobe, demonstrating a self-absorbed nature that Anthony credited to her immaturity. Since he was busy with his scientific pursuits, he allowed her childish behavior until she adjusted to married life.

Since Anthony's father was a powerful duke and cousin to the King, she enjoyed and took full advantage of the prestige that gained her access to the best of England's families. At first, Anthony attributed her insistence to attend every social occasion without him as part of her youthful zeal to experience life. Now as he thought back to that time, he had the distinct feeling, Celeste didn't desire to be encumbered by a husband, she considered boring.

Whatever Anthony's feelings were toward Celeste he did not live up to the principles ingrained in him since birth—to protect those for whom he was responsible. His shameful neglect left him flawed and undeserving. If only he'd been insistent on accompanying Celeste. He could have prevented her death, and been less likely to endure disconnect from his family and the rest of society.

Anthony stalked through the heated press of guests dressed in pretentious silks and satins, jewels dripping from their necks. His mind directed on one objective, his icy gaze parted the crowd. If Rachel was to find a suitable husband, then by God he would make sure her prospects were the finest. Even if it meant his presence at a social entertainment he loathed. Aunt Margaret sat with two old harridans, chatting up a storm. "Where is she?"

His aunt drew herself up, then lifted that dratted ear horn in his face. He repeated his question, and then realized his aunt was going to launch a monologue dating back to the eleventh century's William the Conqueror.

The orchestra stopped for a recess. Anthony wrinkled his nose from the overheated bodies and shrill laughter. A feverish murmur swept through the ballroom. He pivoted and followed their gazes to find *her* moving through the crowd.

The first time he laid eyes on Rachel in his laboratory, Anthony could barely get over her beauty. But this—this was beyond perfection. Both hypnotizing and enchanting, her refinement challenged ordinary souls. Didn't the insinuation of defiance in her unflinching eyes afford her to be that much more bewitching?

The rich, auburn of her hair had been swept up in a gentle swirl, anchored by tiny diamonds. A mass of curls escaped, accentuating her shining blue eyes and arched sable brows. Her willowy figure well-served by a tight-waisted gown, the bodice boasting a row of diamante, plunging low to enhance the deep valley of her swelling breasts. Her pale throat was adorned with a string of diamonds that his father had lent her from the Rutland collection to add sparkle to the deep emerald green of her satin gown.

The sight of her arrested him as well as every hot-blooded man in the room. Delivered to his aunt's side by Sir Martin, Rachel was quickly surrounded by a knot of men. His blood rose in temperature. Two hundred and twelve degrees Fahrenheit, the exact temperature of boiling liquids.

From her clamoring legion of admirers, an older man and his son leaned into her, garnering her attention—overlong—in deep conversation that Anthony doubted had any intellectual acuity. She lifted her chin, and her smile brightened. Anthony viewed the scene through a red haze, and watched as she turned her attentions from one male to another, always smiling and nodding.

She caught sight of him and waved, a daring and refreshing vision of nature and empirical science. She moved to him then, and like a parting of the sea, her demanding admirers, protested the loss of their queen as she left them behind.

"Do you like my new dress?" she whispered

Damn. His mind went awry, his tongue trussed in knots. His body temp scorched a few degrees higher. He could say imposing or stately beauty, no. Goddess-like, yes. Ravishing came to mind. Maybe breathtaking too, because he forgot to breathe for a few moments.

He cleared his throat. "Are you hinting for compliments, Miss Thorne?"

"Would you give me any? No, because you have an economy on words, Lord Anthony. However, I have had so many compliments tonight it would be silly to expect more."

Touché. Miss Thorne didn't just nip; she took a chunk out of him.

Aunt Margaret stood on her cane. "I was remarking on Miss Thorne's popularity. So many gentlemen have promised to call on her. Don't you think she is a grand success, Anthony?"

Like pouring vinegar in a cut.

"Here comes your good friend Lord Ward, and what a colorful spectacle. I am blinded by his scarlet velvet coat and yellow breeches," said Aunt Margaret.

Lord Ward hosted a palette of hues more dazzling than a rainbow. Anthony analyzed the likelihood that Ward's father mated with a peacock.

Although, in deep discussion with another scientist, Ward paused before them, feigning surprise at Anthony's presence. "Oh, Lord Anthony—and the Patriot."

"Good God, a Patriot?" said Ward's companion, Sir Burns, insinuating the Rutland's had invited a pack of rats.

Aunt Margaret glowered. "Her family are loyalists. At no time have they favored measures looking to forcible resistance and independence despite the British government's impolitic and harsh actions disposed on the Colonies," said Aunt Margaret daring Lord Ward and his friend to speak one more insult, she'd shoot them dead.

Regardless of the falsehood, Anthony marveled at his aunt's eloquent support of Rachel and marveled at her sudden ability to hear so well. She fended off a catastrophe.

"My pardon, Lady Margaret," said Lord Ward, "But I was caught in mid-discussion of a scientific matter and made an erroneous slip."

Aunt Margaret projected her horn like a weapon. "Make sure you do not have a *slip* again. I know your grandmother very well. She would have an opinion."

Lord Ward paled. Aunt Margaret didn't just trump Ward, she kicked him in the throat.

"This is serious business," interrupted Ward's partner, Sir Burns, measuring up to the same vanity and buffoonery as Lord Ward. His allusion to Rachel as something nefarious raised the hackles on Anthony's neck.

"I cannot possibly come to a conclusion without supportive corroboration," said Burns.

Anthony scoffed. "Try an educated guess."

Sir Burns gave Anthony a withering stare. "I have degrees from Oxford and Cambridge."

Anthony bowed. "Then try an educated guess, Sir Burns. But you can't because your work is tantamount to a queasy undergraduate scratching his pimples. Everyone knows you are a neck stretcher, copying other students' exams, tossed out of both schools and barely earning one degree."

Sir Burns shook his fist in Anthony's face ready to strike. "You can blow your trumpet all you like, Lord Anthony, but the Royal Society will never shine on your doorstep."

Aunt Margaret leaned in, her ear horn extended between the two men. "Sir Burp, did I hear you say you are working on a strumpet?"

From Aunt Margaret's miscomprehension, everything happened all at once. Face purpling, Sir Burns stalked off followed by Lord Ward. Rachel's lips twitched. Anthony stared at his father's sister.

"I have a practiced eye for concealed disasters." Aunt Margaret repeated the words Anthony had spoken about her in the laboratory. "It's the job of auntie's to interfere and protect their nephews."

Anthony narrowed his eyes. "Your mind is sharper than one hundred axes and your tongue twice as sharp, not to mention how your hearing is selective."

She leaned to listen with her dreadful ox horn. How he'd like to toss the bizarre instrument out the window.

"I'm old. I've earned the privilege of saying whatever I think."

Rachel touched his arm. "Aunt Margaret prevented a brawl."

"My nephew seems to be getting himself in many altercations of late. So unlike you, Anthony. You are always so staid and unadventurous."

Anthony grunted.

"With all humility, I must admit that I'm better than average at clever remarks and have a flair for getting people to dislike me," said Aunt Margaret.

"Not to mention that you could have started a war with your insults to Sir Burp." Anthony tugged at his waistcoat. "Now you have me mispronouncing his name. And with humility?" He choked on that notion.

"Those qualities must be hereditary, don't you think, Miss Thorne?" Aunt Margaret pressed a hand to her chest, and then turned to engage with the older woman beside her. How good she was at chopping him into little pieces.

Rachel giggled. "She is a genius of a woman. Do you think she really needs the ear horn?"

He tipped his head back and downed his drink. "The thought has crossed my mind."

"Captain Johnson, is coming toward us. He is the brother of the recluse whose abandoned home we rode by two weeks ago when you gave me a tour of the estate. He is one of the interesting people I've met this evening. I'll remind you to take care of your remarks. Every time you speak, your mind is on parade."

The sea captain bowed and raised his head like an old turtle, lifting his head out of the sand. "So good to see you again, Miss Thorne, Lord Rutland and Lady Margaret."

Rachel bobbed up on her toes. "I've had a lovely conversation with Captain Johnson this evening. He lives in the village and has invited Aunt Margaret and me to tea."

Captain Johnson pointed with his clay pipe, the bowl of which was a carved caricature of a bearded, turbaned Indian. "Miss Thorne has been charming me with how much she knows of ships. Never met a more knowledgeable female. Interesting, her theories on bilge pumps. And her knowledge on sailing and the seas. Why she could be one of those infamous Colonial privateers."

Anthony choked, thankful Captain Johnson was pulled into conversation by Aunt Margaret before any questions could be asked about Rachel's lineage. An elderly gentleman stepped in front of them and bowed. The din of the crowd prevented Anthony from catching his name.

"Miss Thorne, I have a question on our earlier discussion on some of the plants you described in the New World. Slippery Elm, Witch Hazel and Skull Cap. What again were their medicinal uses?"

Rachel warmed to the topic. "A tea of Slippery Elm is used for intestinal disorders, sore throat, gout and arthritis, we boil the stems of Witch Hazel to treat bruises, swelling and to stop bleeding. Skull Cap is a tonic for the kidney and female complaints."

Anthony looked heavenward. She was an expert in botany?

"Miss Thorne absolutely bewitches me with her knowledge of plants and their medicinal uses. Fascinating, isn't she?"

For the life of him, Anthony couldn't remember who the gentleman was despite his nagging familiarity.

Rachel protested. "I cannot lay claim to the knowledge. Many of the treatments from these plants we learned from the Indians, Mr. Banks."

Joseph Banks. Anthony grabbed a glass of wine from a tray from a passing servant. The president of the Royal Society was in attendance and she had him eating out of her hand?

"And I am not the least bit fascinating," Rachel said, and gave Anthony a quick wink. "Lord Rutland is coming up with something that will be revolutionary. Aren't you?"

"What is it?" Joseph Banks coaxed.

Anthony choked on his drink.

"He cannot tell. Cannot give one hint of his work," she dared to answer for him. "At least, not yet."

Anthony narrowed his eyes. *Wait until I get you home so I can wring your neck.*

"But his discovery will gain him entrance into the Royal Society." She pressed Joseph Banks.

"If his revelation is as sensational as you have mentioned, Miss Thorne, then his entrance is with certainty."

Anthony could not believe his ears. A compliment from the world's most famous botanist?

When he bowed and left, Anthony turned on her. "There you go again, making promises that I may never meet. Don't you know that an entry is voted on by subcommittees of fellow scientists, not demanded by a Colonial? All of England will be laughing at me."

"Don't worry. I have full confidence in your ability."

Anthony growled. "How will that happen, attending tea parties and soirees?"

"Now that we are on that subject. Aren't you glad you came? You have met so many illustrious people."

"Besides you, Joseph Banks, Captain Johnson and Aunt Margaret?" Anthony scanned the room. "The rest were born at the top of the stupid tree and have fallen, hitting every branch on the way down."

She gave him a pained smile—more of a wince. "Being one of the smartest men in the entire kingdom can be a lonely affair. One can imagine when you're constantly surrounded by dimwits, dullards and—worse—those who *think* they're clever."

"Am I the only one not given to bullbaiting and cockfighting?" She pealed out her laughter and everyone looked. He widened his smile, thoroughly enjoying himself, a feat up until now, he'd thought impossible.

Three young gentlemen stopped in front of Rachel, heels together and bending at the waist. "May I have the honor of this dance, Miss Thorne?" The gentleman to the left elbowed in front of the others, yet shied from Anthony's glare. Rachel smothered a giggle.

"Of course, she will," Aunt Margaret intervened. "But one at a time."

"Sir Jenkins, I would be honored to have this dance." Rachel extended her hand to the handsome young man with the trim build, and then gave Anthony a look of laughing exasperation. *I can't help it.* She swirled to the music. Honey scent drifted through the air, the room ablaze with hundreds of beeswax candles in a row of chandeliers that fired hundreds of crystal pendants in a sparkling prismatic display.

She enjoyed a good laugh as much as anyone, and made an effort to bring laughter to others. She could be outspoken, but she also had a teasing nature and a gift for lightening someone's mood, no matter how sour their character.

Sir Davies, her next partner possessed such a disposition. The imperturbability of excess and vanity hung on him like melted wax. Similar to other male acquaintances in England, they lacked goals in life to make a difference in the world and floundered in a sea of indolence.

So unlike Jacob, Ethan and...Anthony Rutland.

Sir Davies smacked his lips. "I have a secret passion, Miss Thorne."

"Passion?"

"May I escort you to a tea with my mother and my aunts' tomorrow? There will be a stimulating discourse on...samplers... my secret passion. Did you know that the tent stitch and cross stitch are the predominant choice in embroidery?"

Sir Davies embroidered? "I-I had no idea." Her skills with the needle were making canvas sails when General Washington needed ships straightaway. Never did she hold the patience for the fine embroidery other women performed and never had she known a man who employed the pastime.

Rachel sighed. Abby had hoped she would find a husband in England. But the men were...not men. If anyone of them had any conflict or confronted any terror, they would run to their snuff-boxes or their mamas in outpourings of hysteria.

Viscount Randall took her hand before Sir Davies had released her. Dressed impeccably, he had a magnificent bleached wig, and charming face decorated with an extraordinary powdered white beard, reminiscent of an ancient sea god. He was not very firm on his legs, his dancing had a shambling, wandering quality and he stepped on her toes more than once.

From over Randall's shoulder, Anthony lounged cynically against the wall, scorn for the couple dancing together. As her new partner turned her, Anthony caught her eye, and she saw his amusement at her discomposure. His eyes flicked from her to Randall and he raised his glass in a mocking toast, as if to wish her well on her husband hunt.

Earlier in the day, she had been disappointed when Anthony had refused to accompany her to the social this evening. But, oh, so joyful when she clapped eyes on him, and for one second, she imagined he came because of her. Remembering his reaction to her new emerald gown, hot torrid heat curled inside her.

Why her dress practically melted off her under his gaze. How he made her feel like a woman, vanishing the girl.

Did Sir Randall say something to her?

"I just came back from Bath. The cure waters are wonderful for consumption," said Randall.

The wasting disease? She widened her eyes in horror.

Davies corrected himself. "I meant to ward off consumption, in case...one was exposed to the lung ailment. Do you do jigsaw puzzles?" He referred to the new pastime of aristocrats putting together cut map pictures of the earth. "I know all about the world."

"Your scholarship astounds me, Sir Randall."

He beamed like an idiot and shook his head as if it were no great feat, and then coughed. Did he have consumption? The powder from his wig fell in an asphyxiating cloud about his face. How she disliked the fashion. Might he die from inhalation of Cyprus powder?

"I would like to call on you in the near future, Miss Thorne."

"Of course," she said, desiring to get away so she could breathe again. The crush was intolerable. So many people in this strange new world, like swimming in a pond and not being able to put your feet down on a stable bottom and getting caught in the muck.

At the end of the waltz, Rachel curtsied. Viscount Randall refused to let her go. She opened her mouth to complain. Many guests watched and she blushed at Randall's offense.

Anthony drew abreast, his face of such dark menace that she shuddered. He jerked his elbow up, grazing Randall's bearded chin and offered his arm. Rachel tugged her fingers away, scathing Randall with an angry glare.

Anthony guided her to the center of the floor for the next dance. "Perhaps you shouldn't be so charming."

She stiffened. "I was not flirtatious."

"I could hold Poseidon's beard and challenge him to a duel."

Rachel huffed, goaded by the mocking amusement in his eyes. "I worried that you'd break his kneecap."

"What would make you think that, Miss Thorne?"

"The fact that Sir Bonneville has been glowering daggers in your backside ever since you arrived, and is sitting with his leg in a splint, propped up on a chair."

"I can't help if Bonneville is clumsy."

Rachel slanted him a knowing look. "You are irredeemable."

"So how is the husband hunt going?"

Rachel started, then shrugged, trying to appear unconcerned when she was not. "Not very well, I'm afraid."

He taunted her with a dubious expression. "I find that difficult to believe when you have so many admirers."

Was he jealous? No. Anthony's concern was steeped in a brotherly nature. "Many have handsome countenances. Baron Jenkins quoted the current price of gold to the ounce. Sir Davies greatest inspiration was having tea with his mother and aunts—and he shared his passion with me."

"Passion?"

"He embroiders."

"Confirms his birth at the top of the stupid tree."

"And Poseidon..." she giggled at Anthony's appropriate reference of Viscount Randall, "...dazzled me with his knowledge of geography, working jigsaw puzzles, informing me, America is to the left—of England."

"Aunt Margaret will have to try harder finding a suitable husband." He whirled her around, his movements, deliberate, with an animal grace.

Rachel's shoulders drooped. She swallowed and looked away, her spirit deflated. "It is folly to believe that I would find someone. I will return to Boston and live as a maid. That is my fate." Never had she really intended to marry anyone in England. She had come only to please Abby and to have a change of scenery. Any idea of marrying anyone of high nobility was impossible. Never would she bring her shame on anyone.

"You will not return until you have helped me with what you promised, Thomas Banks," Anthony said.

Her brain scrambled to find a logical excuse to protest his arrogant demand. But when she raised her face, she was caught in the spell of those compelling blue eyes and clamped down on a sudden temptation to run her fingers over his wide shoulders and muscular arms. The boom of music and clatter of voices disappeared as she forced down those forbidden reactions.

"You have to help me find my unicorn."

In his gruff, growly and roundabout way, he was making up for her disappointment by offering to be part of his discovery. *Oh, Anthony, it is as if I've known you all my life, and when I'm with you, I don't have to pretend to be anyone or anything.*

She knew Anthony Rutland.

Because *she knew* herself.

Pushed behind a wall of painful emotions, trapped in the swirling waters of his subconscious, existed a fear of feeling...and being vulnerable.

Her heart ached for the highly intelligent man who was unable to see how his life paralleled the reclusive Captain Elijah Johnson, the deceased sea captain, making himself into an island... untouched and...isolated. Wasn't Anthony's endless days spent in his laboratory, taking on seemingly impossible challenges, undeterred by failure or setbacks tantamount to the sea captain's hoarding? Preferring to be locked in a sphere of anguish, convincing himself that life proceeds on, undisturbed, for the rest of time?

"You should marry again, Lord Anthony," she blurted, her voice shaking with more emotion than it should.

The dance ended and walking arm in arm, his muscles flexed, a glimmering of wanted touch. Anthony Rutland did not fool her. He wanted to break free of that prison, thirsted for human contact. Teaching him to dip his toe from time to time into humanity's maelstrom was good for him no matter how many times he told her it was illogical.

No doubt he was more entertained than annoyed by what she said.

"Yes, I should. Perhaps you can help me decide whom I should marry."

She winced at his abrupt suggestion. Not at all was she prepared to help him select a wife. But he was offering Rachel trust. She could see it in the warmth of his eyes; hear it in the gentleness of his deep baritone voice. How could she refuse, despite his entreaty cutting her like a knife. Shameful or not, she could not say no and nodded her head, a gesture of sincerity and honesty, she was far from feeling.

Shoved to the side, Rachel looked down on a young woman who had wedged herself between them. Imogene Brougham, the darling of the evening, surrounded by a bevy of female friends and gentlemanly admirers. Rachel pasted on a smile.

Imogene hung onto Anthony and beamed coquettishly. "Do you like the latest French fashion?" She fanned her brocade skirts, "Marie Antoinette's new rage."

An unfamiliar pang of jealousy surfaced. Why? Hadn't she told Lord Anthony they were…like brother and sister? Didn't he own the right to have feminine pursuits and hadn't she just told him he should marry?

With his older brother, the heir, missing and presumed dead, Anthony was fair game. As the prospective next Duke of Rutland, he was a hare before the hounds, a veritable feast for status seeking females on the hunt.

"Do you play the pianoforte, Miss Thorne?" Imogene shrilled, and then looked adoringly to Anthony, one of her hands resting in the region of her heart as though to keep that organ from leaping through the silk of her gown.

Through her lowered lashes, Rachel stole a glance at Anthony's grim expression as he engaged in conversation with the gentleman beside him. She hoped Anthony would marry well. Someone who appreciated him for his talents. *Someone to love him.* Her eyes clouded. She needed him like the very air she needed to breathe, but to dream of a life with Anthony was impossible. He walked a different path than hers.

He would be the next Duke of Rutland. As a duke he would need a match of comparable status. They were an ocean apart.

More young girls circled. Scavengers ready to feed on their prey. He looked incredibly handsome in his black evening attire that fit his tall, muscular frame to perfection. No doubt many of the women yearned to have him at their side, to bask in the aura of restrained power and masculine vitality that emanated from him, and to know the fascination of those bold blue eyes capturing and holding theirs.

All her musings scattered. Festering occurrences of the past tore open old wounds. She was alien, did not belong, a Colonial. "I am not accomplished in that area," Rachel admitted.

"Watercolors? Embroidery? Too bad that you are not refined in the arts." Imogene answered for her. "What can you do?"

"I-I-" Blood drained from her face. What could she say? *That she could climb to the top of a mast in thirty seconds, tie sailor's knots so tight, a ship in a hurricane couldn't breach, discuss hydraulics?* None of which were important to the British social whirl and definitely frowned upon. She lifted her chin. "I'm afraid I do not have any of the refinements you speak of."

To go back to her room at the Rutland's and crawl under the covers. Jacob, Ethan, Abby, her home in Boston...anything to distract.

The girls covered their mouths with their hands in a silent, condemning "no," darting haughty glances to one another. Imogene snorted her disgust and tightened her grip on Lord Anthony. "An English Lord desires an accomplished lady." She conveyed a remote and unapproachable majesty, pouting her perfect lips. Her companions tittered, nodding their heads in undeniable agreement, launching an attack that would have made Cromwell proud, and with Anthony in their sights.

Rachel's world tilted. If Anthony was to be the next duke, Imogene's foregone intimation was valid. Never could Rachel fill that role. He needed someone with a pedigree.

Would Imogene be his wife? Her belly knotted. He deserved so much more. In the past few weeks of working together, they had cemented a friendship, and as a friend, she could not allow Imogene to be that woman. But how?

"Mother, is going to buy me a Shiatsu or should I get a poodle?" Imogene said with all the charm and amiability she could muster. With tactical precision, she squeezed herself between Anthony and the gentleman he was conversing with. Anthony glared. Undeterred, Imogene fluttered her eyelashes as if she had just written and offered him the Magna Carta.

Anthony leaned toward Rachel, brushing her shoulder, his sandalwood drifting through the air. "What do you think about piling our capacitors?

"Is it a kind of cat?" Imogene gushed like water sluicing from a bilge, battling to be in the conversation.

Anthony groaned.

"I'm going to sing tonight, Lord Anthony. Would you be my escort?" Imogene didn't wait for an answer, commandeering Anthony's arm, and all but whisking him away. He stood firm. Imogen jerked back into place. Her eyes protruded. Refusal was not one of her strong points.

Identical to serendipity, a scientific thought occurred to Rachel, bubbling up and popping a champagne cork. "Did you ever think we could use Newton's law to calculate the magnitude of electrical force arising between two charged bodies?"

"Do you sing, Miss Thorne?" Imogene trilled her coup de grace. Her companions raised their eyebrows, expectant of another failed response from Rachel.

"She hums," Anthony answered for her.

To kick him had merit, but in his eyes, Rachel saw a glint of humor, then the amused twitch of his mouth. He was inclined to play games with Imogene.

"Hums? That is not a quality in a well-bred lady," Imogene scoffed.

Anthony scratched his neck. "Rachel, do you remember our conversation about Reverend Pott's wife? Do you recall how she was abated by your singular aim?"

Rachel smiled, abject gratitude from his sardonic sense of humor flooded her. She was scorned by his peers, and he had championed her in a swarm of scavengers.

Imogene glared at them, and then marched off. Her companions raised their noses, pivoted and trailed after their queen.

"A compelling touch of the civilized and the barbaric, don't you think, Miss Thorne?"

"You have managed to be courtly, perfectly mannered and at the same time carry a ducal arrogance that women find irresistible."

"Including you, Miss Thorne?"

There was something in his tone that touched a place inside her. Rachel met his steady gaze, then quickly glanced away before he saw the havoc wreaked on her soul. Was he making another jest?

She couldn't afford to care or indulge herself in emotions that would lead to no end. Keep the relationship on an impersonal level. That was the best way to deal with matters. To put a bit of distance between them had value. A day apart would be best for both of them. Suitors were coming to call, and she'd promised to visit Lord Banfield and Humphrey. How they had championed her the night when Lord and Lady Ward, and then, Sir Bonneville had accosted her. She looked forward to visiting them. There had been a long history between the Duke and her cousin, Jacob that touched her heart.

A day apart would be best for both of them.

Rachel bit her lip. How she hated to disappoint him when he'd been so gallant, but disappoint him she must, and the sooner she spoke the better. With certainty, she was putting too much worry into the situation. Of course, Anthony would be very understanding. "I cannot work in the laboratory tomorrow."

"And why not?"

Her idea was not going to be as easy as she thought. "I have callers visiting tomorrow and I have accepted an invitation with the Duke of Banfield and Humphrey." No need to tell him it was an open invitation.

"You also promised Thomas Banks and the rest of the world something I cannot possibly deliver without a lab assistant. And now you are accepting a company of fools, and cavorting around the countryside." His voice was cold, flat, furious and heard across the room. Revelers craned their necks. If only she could fade into the background.

Anthony proved difficult. "You're invited, too," she proposed in way of a peace offering. "You need to get out more, engage with others."

"You have Aunt Margaret for that." The muscles in his neck corded and his callous tone set the hairs on the back of her neck on end, plain refusing to entertain that her opinion might be valid. "How you like to agree to challenges without thinking them through, and then masking your inhibitions with social seeking. Is this your backward Colonial upbringing?"

Don't cry. Don't cry. Don't cry. "You are stubborn, dogmatic, simple-minded and unable to see—I won't be available the next day, the day after that, and the week after that."

Aunt Margaret sidled up in a whoosh of her skirts, her ear horn bobbing. "I need to go home before I get a headache."

Rachel took Aunt Margaret's arm. Her mother had suffered terrible megrims for hours at a time. "We need to get her home as soon as possible," she commanded Anthony.

Anthony ordered their wraps and coats, bid regrets to their host that they would not be able to attend the soiree. Rachel settled Anthony's aunt into the burgundy velvet squabs of the Rutland coach. Beneath the lantern light, Aunt Margaret appeared hale and healthy, her grey eyes twinkling.

Rachel spoke into the wide end of the ear horn. "I will have Cook make you a special concoction."

"I am saved a headache from Imogene Brougham's singing. The girl has the brain of a toad." Aunt Margaret snorted, her grey eyes shot through with shrewd bright lights of amusement. "Don't let Imogene deter you."

Rachel's jaw dropped. Had Aunt Margaret given her leave on her feelings toward Anthony or was she imagining things? Right now, he was at the top of her lunatic list. The insensitive, hypercritical, tyrant. He was worse than Imogene Brougham and had insulted Rachel to the first degree. Before she could form a reply, Anthony climbed in, slammed the door and stared at her in sullen silence. Aunt Margaret slumped on her shoulder, asleep.

Chapter 9

*R*egardless of the fire roaring in the fireplace of one of the luxurious salons of Belvoir Castle, Rachel pulled her silk shawl about her shoulders to ward off a chill. She turned a dazzling smile to the two gentlemen who had come to call. Despite her bright smile, her mood dipped as she looked through the doorway and out into the hall, hoping Anthony would walk by, even though she knew he'd be in his laboratory. Rachel shivered, wishing she didn't need to separate herself from Anthony. Not only was it for the best, but it was required.

So, why was she so close to tears?

Aunt Margaret chatted with the two gentlemen while Rachel tried to convince herself that her aching disappointment was merely because of Anthony's disagreeable and insulting outburst, but her lonely dejection sprang from something much deeper. She missed him. To see his smile, to be able to work with him again in his laboratory... No. His rudeness was an affront to her New England upbringing and he needed a lesson.

"Miss Thorne, has the unhappy and deluded multitude against His Majesty's forces in the Colonies become sensible of their error?"

She ground her teeth. Sir Alford referred to King George and his cohorts attempt to dismember the Colonies.

Sir Alford thumped his tea cup down on the saucer. "For if all Colonial women are as beautiful as you, we need to conquer the rabble posthaste?"

"The King must make those cloddish rebels suffer the inevitable of England's formidable army," laughed Sir Pembroke.

Rachel's hands clenched over the arms of her chair when Anthony chose to enter the room. She ignored him, incensed by these aristocrats, far removed from what sufferings her countrymen had gone through in the name of freedom. Should she remind them that the rebels were winning? Did she tell them her brother Ethan and formerly, her cousin Jacob robbed the merchant ships along the coasts of England while they slept snug in their beds?

She leaned forward, pretended alarm laced in her voice. "What do you think will happen with the alliance of France and the Colonies, prompted by the British surrender of Saratoga? The French make no secret of providing weapons, munitions and supplies to the patriots. New England is lost to the rebels, including my hometown of Boston. General Clinton's forces have withdrawn from Philadelphia to New York. Is it a matter of time before the British remove from New York? Are the Colonies to be lost?" She held her wrist to her forehead, striking a dramatic pose, and sneaking a glance at her rapt audience. The fools.

Anthony leaned on the mantle and smirked. Aunt Margaret smiled. The other two men sat aghast.

"You must not return to that rabble. The sufferings of those loyal to the Crown, I can only imagine. The King will stop this rebellion." Sir Alford protested, and then turned and frowned at Anthony. "Lord Anthony, so nice of you to join us. Miss Thorne was diverting us with her fears of the rebels."

"She should know firsthand." He smiled a cheerful, self-satisfied smile that put her teeth on edge. "Did she tell you how many ships are produced in Boston?"

Rachel choked on her tea. How dare he reveal her allegiance. "Did I mention that on the ship over here, I observed how cannons were loaded through gun ports and fired with exact precision?"

He inclined his head in acknowledgment and grinned, his eyes lit with intellectual challenge. "In truthful reflections, a *promise* broken can weigh heavy on avenging inclinations."

She widened her eyes. The wretched man lived to intimidate her. She would have none of it. "The nature of one's thoughts could be considered menacing."

"One should not fail in being obtuse," he said carelessly. "Like an arrow released from its bow, your message has met its target, yet your pledge is incomplete."

How she itched to dump her tea on him. Neither life nor death, neither angels nor demons, neither present nor future, nor anything else would make her go back to his lab—until she was ready.

Aunt Margaret harrumphed. Rachel darted a glance to Sir Alford and Pembroke. She let out a breath. The conversation had flown over their heads.

"I will bid you adieu, Aunt Margaret…Miss Thorne." Anthony offered an abrupt bow to her. A barely controlled hostility simmered beneath his formality, if released, would roll her over with the force of a tidal wave. He did not acknowledge the two knights. He turned on his heel and left.

Watching him go, she leaned shakily against the cushions and released a long, shuddering breath. Anthony. A sharp, sweet pain throbbed in her chest. If he knew the truth, he would loathe her.

Chapter 10

*A*nthony slammed the door to the carriage. Rachel had taken their argument seriously and he had to do everything himself. At this speed, he wouldn't make a single discovery until the next millennium.

Fiery acid boiled through his gut. Was she off meeting more potential husbands, buffoons like Pembroke and Alford? What had made him interrupt her visit with those two barnacles? Why did he care who she entertained and why did he possess the juvenile urge to reveal her staunch patriotism? *Jealousy?* Never.

He raked his fingers through his hair, seeking and explanation for his behavior. Because the ramifications of the argument that divided them now threatened to unravel everything he had built. A second later, he realized that was it. The argument.

Not only had his temper brought the miscalculations, but also a tempest of unforeseen challenges forcing him to start over. He had made the mistake of letting his frustration get the best of him and that mistake had dire consequences. To keep his listing ship from capsizing, he would seek her out and apologize. Yes, he would express regret.

He strode past several shops in the village to Harold the Blacksmith's shop. A horse dunked its head into a trough to draw water. He recognized the mare from his father's stables. When the head groom had informed him Rachel had ridden to town on an errand, refusing escort, his blood boiled.

"I've come to pick up my order." He looked around for the infuriating woman. *Running a shipyard.* Clearly, she had enjoyed too much freedom for too long.

Harold lifted his hammer and banged several times on red-hot metal. "It ain't done."

"I need it now." Anthony's stomach muscles hardened, the toothless blacksmith must have taken leave of his senses. To not have finished his order on time?

Harold shoved the flattened metal into a bucket of water. Steam whooshed upward, clouding his blackened face. "Everything is on hold. Have to polish off an order for that Colonial lady."

Colonial lady? Rachel? What was she up to? "Cancel it."

"I can't. I couldn't disappoint her."

So now she had charmed the blacksmith. *Miss Thorne possessed the aptitude to manipulate fools to genius.* "I order you to cancel it."

"She wouldn't like it."

"The devil she will." Anthony was in the mood to take on the blacksmith, had licked him before, but with a hammer the size of Thor's, and biceps the size of trussed full grown turkeys straining his shirtsleeves, he thought better of it. To continue a conversation with Harold was an exercise in idiocy, the blacksmith's mental gears turned only so far.

Anthony stalked off, his heels digging half-moon furrows in the mud. His quarry rested on a porch step, wreathed in a crown of sunlight, sucking on a candy cane and surrounded by several of the village children, also sucking candy canes. Leaning against her was a filthy mutt, dining on fresh meat while she regaled her young audience with stories about Indians in the Colonies. For dramatic effect, she pulled the string of an imaginary bow and sighted down her prey. *Pling.* He could almost hear the whistle of the arrow.

His shadow covered her. Horror written on their faces, the children inched away. *Good.* The mutt barked and the hair on its back ruffled up. She pulled the candy cane out of her mouth and pointed it at him. "Why do you have to be so forbidding?"

"This is my normal face."

"That is your formidable face and would scare the hair off a wooly mammoth." She rummaged through a brown bag and produced six candy canes. "Horehound, peppermint, licorice, lemon… would you like one?"

He bared his teeth. "No. And would you mind telling me what you have the blacksmith engaged in so that he cannot fill my order."

She shrugged a dainty shoulder, daring to dismiss him. "A secret. I gave him my design and told him he had to have it completed immediately. He can shape the copper curvatures that I need."

Damn her conniving heart. He stared her down. "Cancel it."

She scratched the mutt behind the ears and it howled in pleasure. "I like this dog. The blacksmith says he's a stray. Starved you know." She smoothed open the brown paper package so the dog could lick the remnants of his meal.

Anthony grimaced at the two pounds of meat the canine consumed. *Not hungry now.* "We have to talk."

She pasted on the most angelic expression Anthony had ever seen. "About what? She's a very nice companion. The blacksmith said I could have the dog. It's beginning to rain and my horse is in the stables."

"I know—unescorted." He ground out his words. The dog stopped eating and whined.

"Most American women go out unescorted."

"We are not longhouses and savages in England."

"You are behaving like a savage, Lord Anthony. And where is *your* guard?"

"I left without one in a hurry to find *you*."

"Here take a candy cane."

"I don't want one," he shouted. The dog lifted its head, looked at Anthony and ran.

"Now look what you've done. You've scared off my dog."

"Good...why have you ordered the blacksmith to—"

"I didn't."

"He said you did."

"The Duke ordered it."

"My father?"

"He's the Duke, isn't he?"

He'd bite off his tongue before he'd admit to her deliberate attempt to run circles around him. "Get in my carriage before you get wet." He handed her up, followed, and then, clapped the door shut.

"Who is the driver? He looks kind of rough," said Rachel.

Anthony pounded a fist on the carriage to signal the driver. The sooner he got this dispute over with and Rachel back in his lab the better. "The devil I know. Thompson must be out sick. He's the replacement. Quit changing the subject. I have to get my project done and that stubborn blacksmith won't do mine until yours is done."

"There was a strange man in the village. He had that coal dust in the lung kind of cough, the same kind we heard before the flower pot fell on us. He asked questions about your family. Are you sure you don't want a candy cane?"

She wasn't paying attention to one word he said, her head out the window, the mangy dog racing alongside, snapping at the wheels. He rubbed the back of his neck. "I don't want a candy cane. I want—"

"Stop the carriage," she hailed the driver.

"You're not bringing that filthy mutt in the carriage."

With a mutinous glare, she popped open the door and the dog hopped in, yapping, tail-up and nose-dived straight into her lap.

Anthony's nostrils flared. Lavender and Lemon balm mixed with London sewer. "I can't believe it. You allowed that mutt in here against my orders. Out with him."

"Never." She clutched the mud-packed, black beast to her chest mindless of soiling her gown.

He jabbed a finger midair, pointing at her. "My father will not allow him in the house. And I don't want to see the mongrel anywhere near my lab."

"He's hungry and I'm going to care for him."

"You'll have to house him in the stables. I'm allergic to dogs."

She smirked with that *sure you are* look.

Anthony twisted his mouth with derision. She had promised all of England he'd produce something brilliant. "You are wasting my time. Worthless, useless creature." The dog licked her beautiful hand.

"He's very nice. Once he has a bath——"

The horses picked up speed as they left the cobbled road of the village and galloped through the rutted, rain-soaked road. Anthony seized the strap for balance. To think she had gone into town unescorted. Didn't she have any regard for her safety? Disasters gripped his mind. She could have been attacked by highwaymen and been ravaged. Her body left for wild animals. "About the blacksmith..."

"What about him?"

"Stop it. I need him to make copper discs and strands." *She could have broken her neck. He wouldn't have been there to save her.*

The crack of the driver's whip snapped. The horses whickered. The harnesses clanged. The countryside blurred. What was happening to him?

"I don't like your tone and there's nothing to do about it."

Something shattered inside him, driving him beyond rational thought. "You are as useless as that dog. No one would want you."

Her head jerked up. The color drained from her face. "I would not want them anyway."

You fool, he told himself savagely, but the past that tracked him like an ugly shadow came roaring down. He grabbed the sides of his head. No.

"An accident," the gamekeeper said quietly. "Unseated. When Celeste fell...broke—"

"Get a doctor," Anthony said gruffly.

"Anthony, it's no use," his father said.

"Damn you, get a doctor or I'll—"

"Her neck was broken by the fall."

"No—"

"Anthony, she's dead..."

Rachel burst out crying. The dog howled in chorus and she buried her beautiful face in her hands. "Everyone talks behind my back. Do you know how that feels?" Despair leapt from her so profound...she sobbed, her diatribe never ending, but becoming high-pitched, hysterical sputtering of all the wrongs incurred on her and none of which made any sense to Anthony.

His mind clawed for logic. To escape the lunacy that controlled him. He took deep breaths. The fog cleared.

What a brute he'd been. More than a brute. He'd been cruel. *Rachel needed him. Now.*

With certainty, self-pity was an impulse, Rachel seldom tolerated, her New England upbringing forbidding it. Whatever her history was, it had a profound effect on her.

Loud, soulful, hiccupping anguish. "I-I was nearly defiled."

Chapter 11

*N*early defiled? He'd kill the bastard who had dared to touch her.

What a selfish wretch he'd been, thinking of himself when Rachel grieved her own torment.

"You don't know how to love, Anthony," Celeste taunted. *"You only love your isolation."*

The inside of the carriage grew small and suffocating. He rubbed the back of his neck, debating alternatives. Nothing had prepared him for a crying woman. Not just any crying woman, but Rachel. Postulates, theorems, hypotheses, all his old tools left him. He shifted to her side and took her in his arms, allowing a powerful inclination to comfort her as the most natural thing to do. She struggled to break free but he held her tight until she collapsed against him, still sobbing, her head bowed, her body slumped and wetting his shirt with her tears.

How petrifying her secret must have been. How brave she was to tell him.

The rest of the world disappeared with the horror of isolation that taunted him, that constant companion of emptiness. Why did he refuse to push away from Rachel like he had with Celeste?

He needed Rachel. He patted her shoulder to reassure her. "It's okay to cry."

And she did.

No doubt, she cried for the life she could not control, barreling toward the truth with the speed of electrical fire. "I could not grieve because I had to care for my younger brother, Thomas."

Anthony pulled her closer and his jaw ached from gritting his teeth so hard. She referred to when her parents had died.

She shivered and took a deep breath, sinking into the rhythm of her story. "The British controlled Boston and the Quartering Act was executed. I was forced to house and feed His Majesty's soldiers. The same ones who killed my father."

His body tensed. The Quartering Act was a diabolical measure enforced by His Majesty upon the Colonists. But a lone defenseless woman, housing men? He could imagine her terror.

She shook her head, her breath trembling in her chest and rattling through her lips. "I don't know why I'm telling you this."

"Go on. You can confide in me, Rachel," he encouraged, but his voice hardened. Then he spoke more temperately. "I'm listening."

How strong she was to shove away the self-protective veneer she hid behind.

"I was alone, trying to deal with a house full of British soldiers. They knew of my family's patriotic involvement in the war and hated us for it. I was frightened of them—"

Her voice broke. He knew what was coming.

"One soldier, an officer...I felt his eyes on me. When I served his meals, he would find excuses to touch me...I-I complained to his commander but was ignored. The officer would trip Thomas, make my little brother the butt of his sick humor. I had to protect Thomas...my future, a mere whim of British soldiers."

"The mare began to foal. I went to the stable...the soldier followed me...attacked me...I fought...so strong...Thomas came... he tried to save me...so small..." She clutched his shirt, unleashing a flood of desperate gasps, reliving the horror.

"The officer backhanded him across the room...Thomas's head h-hit a block and tackle...he paid the price. If only I hadn't gone to check on the mare, Thomas would be alive. Little Thomas, barely nine summers, so full of love and mischief and life. He died, protecting me. Why didn't I die instead?"

Envisioning her helplessness, Anthony balled his hands into fists. A howling wind threw rain against the window in strong gusts, and the air hung heavy and cold as stinging nettles.

"The British officer renewed his attack on me, knocked me unconscious. From what I learned later, Jacob arrived, beat the officer. Other soldiers arrived. The officer who attacked me accused Jacob of murder. Who was to take the word of a drunken Colonial against one of the King's men?

Jacob was arrested and dragged away in chains. Incarcerated and awaiting trial, he faced execution. I lay in a coma for many weeks, unable to aid his defense. Everyone knew the charges were ludicrous. With the help of Patriot's, Jacob escaped. Because of me, he had to leave Boston, and then took up the dangerous practice of privateering."

"When I awoke, people treated me like a social pariah. Men who had loved to dance with me..." she shrugged. "...dropped off. All I ever wanted was a husband and children..."

She pushed away from Anthony, but he held her solid.

"I-I don't deserve anyone's affection...I am not worthy."

Because I'm not that desirable.

Now he understood. Anthony wanted to pummel his fists into the bastard officer's face, to beat him to a bloody pulp.

The horrors she had been drawn against. That this bright, beautiful woman had suffered so much. In rapid succession, the death of her parents, the impressment of British soldiers, no family to protect her, the death of her baby brother before her own eyes. How one vulnerable girl had faced a world gone mad. He cursed his countrymen, the sore need and greed of men for power over the Colonies.

He offered her his handkerchief. "Dry your tears," he said with gentleness, far from the roar he forced down in his throat.

The stinging grief and crushing guilt, she suffered, had never abated. The yoke of responsibility in protecting her brother, followed by his murder, weighed a lodestone around her neck. No wonder she withdrew at times. No wonder she felt unworthy. Deep down, beneath that glowing smile was a magnificent woman who held an ongoing sense of helplessness, bearing the weight of everyone dear to her.

He rubbed his chin in the silkiness of her hair. The dog lay on the opposite seat, head sagged between her paws, and eyes lifted in empathy. "I'm glad you told me. It wasn't your fault. You didn't cause it and you didn't deserve it."

Rachel's lingering self-condemnation from the failed rape and the stigma attached haunted Anthony. In England the disgrace would be bandied about with ruthlessness, but puritanical Boston Colonials? She'd have been crucified.

To exhibit the tremendous strength and courage she had, striving to do good, to push away her pain and sufferings, and then she did everything in her power to protect others. That she faced the humiliation of a tyrannical British officer. That she rose from the ashes to take over a shipyard, a job for men. That she championed him at Lord Chelmsford's. That she put up with his stubbornness and impatience, demonstrated she was beyond an angel...and she cried for the profound loneliness that filled her heart, and a future that seemed bleak and uncertain.

Rachel's kindness to his favorite aunt said a lot about her character. Many of the women of his acquaintance were like Celeste. They would have been unaware of an old woman's comfort, covering Aunt Margaret with a blanket while she slept. Polite but haughty, and with certainty, never would they have exercised the compassion Rachel did.

She touched his soul. Anthony held her, the painting in the library of God and his angels came to mind. "The experiences of our past are the architects of our present. Do not let the bad overwhelm what is good. Sometimes, suffering out of our control marks us but need not scar us for life. What we allow the mark of our suffering to become is in our own hands. You are nothing but goodness, Rachel."

She unleashed another floodgate of tears. Oh, dear Lord, he wasn't any good at this at all. "I'm sorry. I didn't—"

Rachel buried her face in his neck and sighed, her wet lashes brushing against his skin with every blink.

"If anybody's opinion matters, it is yours, Anthony."

Pride burst in him. He traced the smoothness of her chin, lifting her face to meet his, slowly, lazily, never breaking eye contact, he leaned forward and in one smooth movement kissed her. Her sweet breath warm against his mouth, the softness and pliability of her lips against his, and then unspoken promises that rocked him in a way he wouldn't have believed.

Their lips parting, she said, "Why did you do that?"

He was breathing hard and so was she. "I don't know. It seemed the logical thing to do."

On all fours, the mutt growled, stuck its head out the window, full blown barking, running back and forth on the opposing seat… wouldn't stop. "I should muzzle the mutt."

The carriage pitched. Catapulted into the air, rolled and thumped and bumped. Rachel screamed, slammed into Anthony. The carriage came to a standstill. He rather liked her on his lap except the carriage slanted at a ninety-degree angle. What stopped them? He yanked the curtain back. Rachel moaned. Plus or minus a few inches, a frigid river churned two hundred and eighty yards below.

"Don't move. The rotted log that supports us will snap under the stress." He calculated the odds of dying by falling on one of the many sharp protruding branches that dotted the cliff like pikes, as opposed to fracturing their skulls on razor-sharp rocks that jutted out in the river. Not good. No need to inform Rachel of the danger. As likely as not, she had the formula worked out ahead of him.

On the cliff, up above, the dog barked. Must have been thrown from the carriage. The driver shouted and hooves clattered down the road. The driver had taken off with the horses.

No help from that quarter. Clearly another attack. "Are you all right?"

The carriage slipped, caught again. Rachel shrieked, clung to his jacket. "We need to depart this death trap."

"I'll stay here and balance the weight. You climb out the top window."

"I can't leave you here."

"Go. I'll climb after you."

She hesitated then crawled out the window, grappling roots and ledges, hauling herself up the slope. The log popped. The carriage slid. Taking him down. He thrust with his feet, dove out the window. Hooked his arm on an overhanging branch, swinging wildly.

Rachel scrambled down, dug her feet into a frozen crevice, held out her hand. "Now."

Newton's law of motion: A body will stay in motion unless acted upon by an unbalanced force. Anthony swung his full weight, clenched her outstretched hand. The inertia of her yank and the shift of his mass equaled his impact into the rock face. His breath whooshed out. His jaw throbbed. Stopped by Newton's unbalanced force was like getting hit with a team of horses, yet arguably, a good place to be.

A rumble like thunder followed by a loud crash. He followed her glassy stare to where the carriage rested spiked on rocks in the river. Icy water rushed and flooded the conveyance, the underbelly exposed to view.

"The axle has been sawed." She started shaking.

Anthony held her close until her trembling stopped. "Other than a few scratches, we are good."

The dog whined and barked. "At least she is safe," Rachel smiled.

His Rachel was back. Anthony pushed her up the crag, and in minutes, they hauled over the top of the cliff. The driver and horses had vanished. The dog leapt into Rachel's arms, licking her face.

"Someone is trying to kill *you*, Anthony." She put the dog down and faced him. "I told you that I didn't like the look of the driver."

She didn't mention that she could have been killed, unselfishly concerned for his well-being. Her skirts were soaked with mud, her auburn hair undone from its pins, flowed in riotous waves down her shoulders and back. She couldn't have been more beautiful.

"We have a long hike, and if you say, I told you so...well, I deserve it one hundred times over." He held out his arm and she grabbed hold. He led her down the mud-rutted road as if they were entering an evening opera instead of following the track of the Rutland's stolen horses.

"We need to focus on what happened." Her tone was firmer now, conjuring memories with that precocious mind of hers. "I need you to think. Have you seen the driver before?"

"I was in a hurry to find you. I didn't pay attention to him."

Rachel let out a long slow breath, her expression grave. "He was six feet, brown straw-like hair sticking outside his hat, blue watery eyes and unshaven. Then there was the strange man who approached me in town. He had that voice—I would never forget—and I'm sure it was the same raspy vocal sounds in tenor and octave I've heard before. He had a red wool cap, probably concealed a bald head, thin frame, nose like an ape, wart on his upper right cheek, five foot, eight inches tall, red coat. Anyone familiar?"

She had a great memory for detail. He rarely remembered a face. "Could be five percent of England."

"What kinds of questions did he ask?"

"He asked of you, what you were working on in your laboratory...if I had heard that the laboratory had exploded. He had laughed at that notion. I told him he was rude and should frame his questions to the Rutland's and then I walked into the store to get away from him. When I turned to get a better look, he had disappeared."

Anthony shook his head. "I suspect he was the one responsible for sawing through the axle. The driver, I've never laid eyes on him."

"Why would the man asking the questions, risk being seen?"

"To gloat. A farewell performance before sending us to the next world. With certainty, he didn't plan on us surviving."

She wiped a smudge on her cheek clean with her sleeve. "And how many do you estimate are there working together?"

"To saw the axle took a while and the culprits were cunning enough to calculate the break at the time we would be travelling along the river."

"Someone in the town was witness to their machinations," she insisted. "Unless they performed the deed in your stables?"

Leave it to Rachel to be thinking ahead of him. "That would take a lot of daring in light of the extra guards posted. Which reminds me, do not leave the premises unless you are escorted. I command it. Your association with the Rutland's has endangered you, especially now that you can identify someone, possibly the villain himself. He will be more desperate."

She raised two fingers to her forehead and gave him a jaunty salute. "Aye, aye, Captain."

He scowled. "Today's activities could have yielded ghastly consequences."

Rachel snorted. "Even in your most serious glare, you are nothing but a pussycat."

"Have you asked Sir Bonneville about his knee?" Anthony said.

Rachel's ring of laughter wound through the forest and her good humor was infectious.

"I deserved that, Lord Anthony."

He wanted to kiss her, again, right then and there. *I'm no good at this...romance and attachments. I'm a disaster. I don't know how to love.* He'd kissed her in the carriage, but that was impulsive. He hadn't known what else to do to comfort her. Hah. If only, he believed that. Truth was, he kissed her because he'd wanted to. He was drawn to her like the proverbial moth to the flame.

His muscles tightened. She had suffered tragedy after tragedy, grieving overlong and faced the hopelessness of an uncertain future. That she had been subjected to ridicule and scorn for a violent act entirely against her and out of her control was unconscionable. How he'd like to make it up to her. But how?

"You know what I'm dreaming about?"

Locking yourself up in my lab with me. Forever. "I haven't a clue. Enlighten me."

"Having a whole plate full of cream puffs. My stomach is caving in."

"After today's ordeal you can have all the creampuffs you want." He wanted to kiss her and go on kissing her forever.

"I am going to keep you to your promise."

Scattered across the forest floor remained the heart-shaped leaves of heliotrope. In between, patches of snowdrops showed their snowy white flowers, an indication that the shorter days began to lengthen. Blue tits abandoned their communal flocks and were feeding in pairs, their soft *tupp* echoing through the woodland canopy. Two squirrels emerged, chattering, and scolding, driving two birds to a higher branch. The dog chased after them, barking at the bottom of the tree. He smiled at the scene. "Lovely," he whispered, looking down on her.

How odd. With Rachel, he seemed to notice things. Things he hadn't noticed in a long time.

Dusk approached and with it, leaden gray skies unburdened freezing rain, falling over his collar, the icy chill, cascading down his back. Rachel's teeth chattered and he hated that she was exposed to the elements. He took off his coat and draped it over her shoulders. If only he could conjure a ride home.

"What else can go wrong?" she said as they rounded a bend in the road. The dog growled and the hair ruffed up on its back.

"That's far enough," a gruff male voice came from behind.

Guns drawn, two men with scarves, concealing half their faces moved from the woods. The dog snarled and snapped. Rachel called her back and she leaped into her arms. Not a great guard dog.

Highway men? Unbelievable. Anthony pushed Rachel and the dog to the left, shielding her with his body. They halted behind a felled tree, the southern end, closest to Rachel, projected upward at a thirty-degree angle. A delightful boulder rested midway beneath.

Rachel blinked the sleet off her lashes. "Are you jesting? In this weather?"

"We want to unload you of your baubles."

"I would if I had any valuables." Anthony fumed. He had enough of this day.

East Londoners, the way they dropped their *r-r's*. A long way from home. Must be desperate to adopt new hunting grounds, except their trade must be good because the fat guy was well fed. The men clicked the flintlocks on their guns. Sixty percent odds their powder was wet and the firearms were useless.

The smaller one chortled. "By their fancy dress, Gus, I'm guessin' they have lots of money."

"Fool. I told you not to say my name."

"Sorry, Gus."

"Shut-up." Gus motioned Anthony with his gun. "Hand 'em over."

Anthony hedged, his head down, fumbling in his pockets for money. "Are you part of the group that tried to assassinate us earlier?" Their scarves had slipped, revealing their faces. Not the sharpest knives in the drawer. What was worse, the dolts would have to kill them since he and Rachel could now identify them.

Anthony tracked to the right, six feet down the log. In the event the highwaymen were trigger happy, and the forty percent chance the powder did work, he'd draw the fire away from Rachel. He faced Gus, looming up out of the gray gloom. His companion smiled, flashing a row of three rotten teeth. *Brothers?* Up close, the corpulent Gus was more ominous. Nothing like the farm boys he boxed. Those boys were immense, calm and purposeful and above all, totally in control of their brains.

Gus's neck swiveled back and forth on powerful shoulders, the kind of shoulders that could easily lift an ox. "What do you mean... assassinate?"

"Sawing the axle on the Duke of Rutland's carriage, precipitating the conveyance's fall down a cliff, the intent to kill me and the lady. Hanging for attempted murder."

Gus hopped from side to side, bending one way, bending the other. His huge feet stamped divots in the mud. The dog leaped from Rachel's arms, charged the giant. Gus kicked her and the mutt went squealing into the woods.

Rachel started toward Gus. Anthony raised a hand to warn her down. *He's mine.*

"Did you have to kick her?" she shrieked.

"The damn dog bit me," Gus sneered. "I don't know about any carriage."

Anthony believed them. These two couldn't handle a saw let alone plan cutting an apple in half. "Highway robbery is another offense, bearing severe penalties. Of course, you can only be hanged once. I'll give you two options. Option one is agree right now to let us go, and I'll forget about the robbery."

Three-Tooth sneered. He was the furthest thing from Gus, convulsing with spasms. Definitely unstable. His eyes were like hot coals buried in snow and his lower lip hung down his chin as if pulled between here and London, and then snapped back. "What is option two?"

"I recommend option one."

Both men looked at each other, and then at Anthony. "You're a raving lunatic. But because you are so polite and entertaining, we'll end your life quick with a bullet to the head," said Gus.

Two against one was never a problem. Except he had Rachel to consider. Three-Tooth... he'd take down first. Gus—like chopping down an oak tree. Where would he start? An incoming elbow to his throat? A short left to the back of the kidney?

Rachel whispered. "They have guns." She dipped her eyes to the log. Her reckonings on par with his. *Good.*

"Yeah. We have guns," Gus said which gave Anthony a glimmer of hope because Rachel likely reminded the pair that they had guns. Hard as it was to suffer their stupidity, Anthony felt sorry for them. Unfortunately, their lack of intelligence bolstered their confidence.

"Hand over the goods. My gun hand is getting jumpy," Gus instructed.

"Wait," said Three-Tooth. "He hasn't told us option two."

Definitely hereditary. Anthony assessed the likelihood that the mother was the sister of their father. He'd bet his laboratory that the event was not random, even up the ante, by tossing in his bank account. A useless gamble, no return on his wager.

Anthony sighed. "Option two—you don't get hurt."

Gus choked on his drool. Triple-Tooth snickered. Anthony sidestepped once more. Not that he wanted to get away from the stench of unwashed bodies, and rum, but wanted a clear path over the tree before he made his move.

Rachel shrieked. "I told you that we shouldn't have gone to town today. First, I was thrown over a cliff, and now I'm robbed at gunpoint. This is all your fault. What can I expect from a half-witted, addlepated fool? Why I should tar and feather you."

What the hell was she doing?

On and on she went, throwing all kinds of epitaphs on his person. Enough to make a sailor blush *and*. . .to distract the highwaymen. Smart girl.

"The lady has it in for you." Gus snorted, his best imitation of a laugh.

Anthony turned to her. "Rachel, what do you think of a tangent of a thirty-degree angle in repose, and then mathematically expressed by mass equaling force times distance?" he asked, raising the stakes on her ruse.

She edged toward the raised part of the log, and shook her fist at him. "Only a buffoon would ask me that. Based on Archimedes principal where the force applied at the end points of the lever is proportional to the ration of the length of the lever measured between the fulcrum and application point of the force applied to that end."

Three-Tooth scratched his lice. "What's she talking about?"

She hiked her skirts to her knees. Anthony swallowed, forced himself to think. The highwaymen's mouths dropped open, engaged with her lovely legs.

Right where Anthony wanted them.

Three things happened simultaneously. Rachel jumped on the high part of the log. Her full weight and inertia pitched the opposite end with enough force to throw back the highwaymen. Guns sailed into the air. A pistol fired, the ball colliding with the treetops, showering a spray of splinters and twigs. Anthony sprang over the debris, hit the gaping Three-Tooth in the mouth. His teeth went flying. The runt of the litter crumpled into the leaf mold. Three-Tooth would have to be renamed. One-Tooth was more appropriate.

Gus came at him, eyes wild, launching a right. Anthony ducked, the buzz swept over his head. Gus's momentum carried him in a curve, his kidney exposed for the taking. Easy enough, a question of force, the product of mass times velocity squared. Anthony hit a short right, a colossal blow, a blow that would have cracked a stable beam. Gus stumbled and bent viciously backward from the force of the punch, the breath whooshing out of him. No doubt, the shock hitting the back of his lungs like a million tiny needles, heated red-hot in a fire. He tottered, and his right leg went stiff.

He didn't fall like a normal person. No, a normal person would have been ready to be buried six feet under. Instead, he trembled like aspen leaves in the wind, then, grinning the hulk of a man righted himself and lunged. Apparently, rum numbed his pain, and emboldened his attack. Anthony smashed his fist into Gus's jaw, but his foot slipped in the mud. Not like boxing in the barn with a solid floor beneath his feet. As he straightened, Gus slammed a punch to Anthony's chest, the force enough to knock a horse into paralysis. He gasped and whooped, his lungs collapsing. Gus swung another right and left, but Anthony raised his fists batting off the jabs. He ducked and danced to the side, and then advanced, unleashing the full force of his blows. Two, four, six jabs. His adversary breathed hard his gloating grin faded, blood poured from his mouth.

"I thought you said you could fight," Anthony taunted.

Gus roared after Anthony head on, landing savage thrust after thrust of his fists. Anthony recovered with a swift, sudden spin borne of instinct. Gus backhanded Anthony across the forehead. Breathing hard, drifting in a fog, Anthony kept punching...survival...he hammered Gus again and again...and the guy was still standing.

He who has the higher ground is the victor. Sun Tzu, an ancient Chinese warlord advised his military leaders to take the higher ground and let the enemy attack from the vulnerability of a lower position. Must force Gus to the ground.

Dizzy and losing his balance, Anthony spun, smashed his heel into the kneecap of Gus's good leg, felt the bone crack through his boot. Like Bonneville, the Goliath went down, too...but then, his big hands clawing at the earth, Gus raised up crawling toward Anthony...one last attempt. Anthony tried to shake the cobwebs from his head, rubbed the dirt from his eyes and clenched his fists, but Gus was almost upon him. And then...the giant slumped face forward into the mud.

Anthony wiped the blood from his mouth...and did a double take. Like an Amazon goddess, Rachel stood poised over Gus, a rock in her hand, ready to strike again.

"Enough of you two playing games."

Anthony cleared his head and stood, tipped his toe against the big man's body. Unconscious. *"Games?* I'm lucky I'm not fodder for the worms." The dog yipped at his feet and Anthony bent down to pat the beast's head.

He angled his head to the rock she dropped. "So primitive." Anthony remarked drily. "Too bad you didn't have your bow and arrow."

"I have been reduced to rocks. And if you say, 'how typical for a Colonial,' I'll hit you with a rock."

"We need to tie them up. Can you spare your petticoat?"

"Turn around," she ordered him.

With reluctance, he let go and presented his back, remembering long perfect legs. "Where has the sudden modesty come from? I seem to recall you hiking your skirts up—"

"That was a distraction and you know it was. And if you ever tell anyone, I'll—"

"Hit me with a rock. I'll shall tremble in my boots from the thought."

"You can turn around now."

After tearing her petticoat in strips, she instructed him on impressive sailor's knots, foolproof in securing their assailants.

She stopped a few steps away from him, gazing at him in fear and confusion, as if she wanted to come the rest of the way, but couldn't. He took the last few steps, enclosed her in his arms, trying to ignore the incredible feel of her crushed against him. He wanted to kiss her but she was trembling so violently that he was afraid to knowing her history. Instead, he just held her with her face cradled against his chest and slowly stroked her long, lustrous hair. Rivulets of sweat and blood poured down his temple and his jaw hurt like hell, but all felt right with the world.

"You saved my life again. You make me feel protected."

In that moment, he found a thousand things that he loved about her.

Very slowly and gently, Anthony lifted her chin and kissed her. He kissed her long and *lingering*, with all the aching tenderness in his heart, and she laid her trembling fingers against his cheek and began to kiss him back.

Her soft lips parted with only the slightest urging from his probing tongue into her mouth, and then she gave him hers. He teased her, tormented her, offered himself to her by thrusting deep with his tongue, then retreating and thrusting again and again, until Rachel was clinging to him, her mouth moving back and forth over his in passionate surrender to the wild, erotic kiss.

Shivering and tentative, she pressed her form into him, his jacket that she wore, opened and her full breasts flattened against the wet silk of his shirt. Shyly, she moved her hands up his chest, and without guile, her fingers continued upward until they stroked the dark hair at his nape. Stunned by the force of the need pulsating through his blood, he had to stop this madness before it went any further, before he pinned her to the mud like a beast. Rachel was his sister's friend. Stop. *Now.*

Growling from deep in his throat, he tore his mouth away and stared into her passion-drugged eyes. "I have to end this before I do something I regret." He touched her cheek with his forefinger, tracing the elegant curve of her cheekbone. How he adored her spirit, her freshness. She was warmth and awakening passion, headstrong and sweet, loyal, intelligent and witty. *His pearl beyond price.*

The rumble of a wagon, thundering around the bend caused them both to turn. The dog snapped at the wagon's wheels until the driver braked his team. It was one of his father's trusted tenants.

"Lord Anthony? Heard a gunshot." He narrowed his eyes at their tied-up quarry. "Glad I wasn't at the end of those fists of yours. Happy I came along. I imagine you'll want help, throwing them in the back and a ride home."

Chapter 12

*T*he horrid events of the past few hours surfaced a new kind of panic. That she had revealed the secret of her near defilement to Anthony. That he had kissed her. Suddenly she wanted to dive beneath the covers of her bed, plant a pillow over her head and force out the chaos surrounding her. Pretending that she had no time for emotion, for grief, for guilt, for responsibility, only the crisis facing the Rutlands to block the dissonance of her thoughts.

If that could ever happen.

She had taken a bath, changed into a clean dress, and now welcomed the radiating warmth of a stoked fire in the library to thaw out her bones. Aunt Margaret snored in a wingback chair. To tuck her toes beneath her skirts and join Anthony's charming aunt had appeal for she was barely able to keep her eyelids open.

"The highway men are being questioned. One of my hired guards was a former army sergeant and very good at convincing them that the accuracy of their truth is critical," said the Duke, his voice firm and solid.

"I don't think you will get much out of them," said Anthony. "They didn't seem to know about the carriage, but maybe they witnessed something that might prove helpful."

"What did the man in the village who accosted you look like?"

The Duke pulled Rachel from her musings. Adding details, she'd forgotten, she restated his description. "He had a skeletal face and his body seemed wasted away, red cap, a coarse Simian nose that sniffed every which way for wandering odors, moist black eyes that protruded out of pouched pockets and darted all over the place."

Anthony nodded, his aquiline jaw working in frustrated circles as though chewing on a thought. "Any of your tenants who fit that description?" he asked his father.

"Not one that I can think of," said the Duke. "I will have someone investigate."

"Could it be——" Rachel pulled Anthony back to the past.

"Interesting," Anthony nodded.

"I'm not following," said the Duke.

"A relative of Percy Devol, the man who had kidnapped Abby?" Anthony explained. "You think the culprit who sawed the axle——"

"Sure...strangely and——" She stopped short, his meaning registered. "Killed your assistant?"

"It would explain a lot," Anthony said. "I've been thinking of the precision of the carriage axle being sawed...how long it had taken, over rough roads, someone had timed it before, practiced it even.

Puzzled by this last point...how long had it taken, Rachel asked, "And where did the coach driver go? What about the stable master?"

"The stable master was found tied up in the back of the stables," said Anthony's father. He received a whack on the head and was out cold. He didn't see or hear anyone."

The butler came into the room followed by a footman with trays of hot tea, scones, sandwiches and a large plate of cream puffs.

Dreaming of the delicate pastry, Rachel eyed the arranged plate, her stomach rumbling with an unladylike sound. She groaned. Even a crumb would be a feast.

"As you wished." A sliver of knowing mischief slipped into his smile, and her heart increased in tempo.

The footman poured her tea into a delicate china cup, the loveliest shade of cobalt blue and bordered with a bright gold.

When the footman finished serving, the Duke nodded for his dismissal.

Sebastian, the butler closed the doors and returned.

"Please tell us what you have learned, Sebastian," said Anthony's father.

"Your Grace, there is not much we were able to get from the highwaymen. They are East Londoners, had nothing to do with the carriage accident, or George's demise. The sergeant was very thorough. The territory they employed for their nefarious business dealings in East London proved competitive, forcing them to search new and available pickings, on your estate. The ill-fated circumstance was that they ran into Lord Anthony. No one local would have taken on his lordship."

"Thank you for your confidence, Sebastian," said Anthony.

Rachel agreed. Anthony could fight. That savage masculine face, all angles and cleverness and startling blue eyes. Handsome except for the black and blue bruises that swelled, both repugnant and compelling. The odds set against him, outgunned and outmanned, and how he had dispatched them—this Anthony was not the man she had met before. A thrill of danger brushed her spine, and at the same time, she squelched the urge to sit next to him and comfort him. He nudged a crystal dish of butterscotch pudding toward her.

She stared at his beautiful face and beautiful lips. Magic and wonder all rolled into one. *What would you do Lord Anthony if I kissed you?*

"The guards caught a man in the trees bordering the castle, but he was here to see one of the housemaids," Sebastian added.

"I'll alert the tenants to keep their eyes and ears open, post more guards. With this situation, none of us are safe," growled the Duke.

Rachel took her first bite of the buttery sweet pudding that melted in a mélange of spices on her tongue. She couldn't help but savor the confectionary taste of what had looked like an unassuming dish. "We arrive at the same deduction then."

"Meaning?" Anthony cocked his head, and Rachel could sense the wheels turning. He shifted his gaze to her lips, and then back to her, his eyes wide. "You think—"

"Meaning that it confirms our conclusions of someone with influence and a lot of money is involved."

He dropped three cream puffs on her plate.

Rachel stared at him like he'd lost his mind. She picked up a cream puff and took a bite. An errant pearl of white cream escaped and she chased it back into her mouth with the tip of her finger. Anthony caught her breach in etiquette. The lighting in his eyes went from grey to deep blue. Her stomach erupted in a flurry of moths, raining memories of the way he'd reached for her in the carriage and kissed her and then again right after they had been held-up by the highwaymen. Like a man in the desert who reaches for water. She liked that thirst.

"The dog has been given a bath, fed and resides in the stable. She is happy in her new home." Rachel melted. Anthony had given her a little bit of sunshine and hope in a world of shadow and pain. She breathed easier since she had confessed to Anthony of her past and felt better because of the declaration. This interlude in time she would always remember and wanted to savor.

He shrugged. "It seemed appropriate."

Aunt Margaret sat up and blinked. "I must have fallen asleep. You two look so tired. You should retire."

Rachel needed no prodding, swaying as she stood.

Anthony rose to steady her, "I believe we have exhausted everything there is to say. I will escort, Miss Thorne upstairs."

Sebastian peeked through the doors, and then closed them. "They are upstairs, Your Grace."

The Duke raised his brandy snifter, rolled the amber liquid around in the crystal. "Do you think the romance is advancing?"

Aunt Margaret tilted her grey head. "Of course it is. Didn't you see how Miss Thorne darted glances at Anthony like she wanted to get up and fuss over his bruises? Didn't you see how Anthony insisted on escorting her upstairs as if she were the most precious thing in the world?"

The Duke reared, thunderstruck. "I missed that."

She looked down her nose. "Most men would, so don't feel left out."

Sebastian coughed.

"Have you worked out a deal with Miss Thorne to build her invention?" Margaret demanded.

Wasn't he the Duke? How Aunt Margaret loved to command. She still thought of him in his nappies, yet he had to admit, her battle instincts were inspiring and——remarkable. "I engaged her to do the job as a quid pro-quo for the wardrobe, but keeping them apart, how can we keep the attraction going?"

"Thought blackmail beneath you, Richard. You have surprised me with your resourcefulness." With all the benevolence in the world, she gave him a firm nod.

Should he genuflect?

"To answer your question, the mysteries of attraction cannot be explained through logic."

The Duke flicked his gaze upward. "Abby said they were meant for each other, and I concur with her thoughts. Anthony has come out of his shell, and I would buy Miss Thorne a thousand wardrobes. I can't thank her enough."

"She is magic," said Sebastian. "A delight to have around, if I may say so, Your Grace."

The Duke sipped his brandy. "I will do anything to get her in the family. They are the same, yet uniquely different."

Aunt Margaret tapped her fingertips together. "Sometimes the fractures in two separate souls become the hinges that hold them together."

"But with all this chaos. The sawed carriage wheel has yet to be investigated. Where was the carriage, who was near it today? Then there is the problem of Anthony's murdered assistant, the two highwaymen. How can a relationship develop?"

Aunt Margaret displayed a playful grin. "Courage and perseverance are the magic amulet before which complications disappear and obstacles vanish into air."

"I wish I had your confidence."

Aunt Margaret snorted, "Doesn't everyone."

Chapter 13

Would it work? Rachel placed her hands on her hips. A week of labor had gone into her project. Her masterpiece was complete. A maid scurried in, depositing an armload of towels, soaps and fragrance oils to stock the new bathing chamber. Rachel shooed the curious maid and workmen away, locking the door behind them. She bit her lip. The initial test had to be performed alone.

A bronzed cistern filled with water had been positioned to the rear of the kitchen fireplace. Cook tended the duo-functioned fire that allowed her to heat the cistern water and to cook the meals for the day. Due to the Duke's insistence and largesse, Rachel had improved her earlier pump design. A kitchen boy, employed to work the copper and elm chain pump, stood at the ready. She tapped the pipe, sound waves, traveled down the installed conduits to the kitchen, signaling the pumping to start. She held her breath. *Please work. Please work.*

Crackle. Glug. Whoosh. Like magic, water sluiced into the tub from the blacksmith crafted, copper spouts. She clapped her hands together, pure joy erupted from the bottom of her toes, bubbled in her stomach to the top of her head.

What a shame Anthony was not there to share in her triumph. But, he had been warned away and everyone had been sworn to secrecy until she had worked out any flaws. Her pride was at stake. He was taking it very bad, like a bear with a thorn in its paw, complaining no one was helping him in the lab. The cook had even caught him snooping in the kitchen.

How she missed his strong arms about her, wanting him morning, noon and night. How many times had she fantasized kissing him, smelling his hair, the touch of his breath on her face...his hands on her? She wiped her damp palms on her skirts. A longing grew like she never felt before. She shook her head. No. *Do not yearn for what you cannot have.*

When the tub filled sufficiently, she tapped the copper pipe, signaling the pumping to cease. Her footsteps amplified across the marble floor as she walked around, admiring the tempting copper gleaming tub. This was her child, her design. Why not try it out? *Should she?* Rachel swished her hand through the warm water, the temptation drawing on her like the earth's gravitational force. She glanced at the window, the door, and a smile formed when she touched the water again, and a small moan escaped. In seconds, she unfastened her dress, undid her laces, and took off her stockings.

Her dress fell to her ankles in a soft hush. After pinning up her thick hair, she stepped into the tub, lowering herself, and allowed the fragrant water to lap about her shoulders. At last, she picked up a cake of lavender and lemon balm soap and smoothed the satiny bar over her skin. The scent wafted, lulling her as she rested her head against the tub. How she wished she could stay here longer. A lot longer when she thought of Anthony and their passionate kisses.

Her heart sank. In a short time, she would voyage to Lisbon, Portugal, a neutral port for American and British ships. Her three months were over. Ethan would pick her up for the long voyage back to Boston. Aunt Margaret and the Duke had begged her stay. But the only thing more inconceivable than leaving was staying. And the only thing more unbearable than staying was leaving. To watch Anthony court and walk another woman down the aisle? The inevitable was intolerable. To think of him in another woman's arms was unbearable. But his life was hammered in stone, that he must marry, and he needed someone to enhance the ducal title—not a Colonial.

She lifted a leg above the water to rub the soap all the way down to her toes. She tapped the pipe again and the pump started with a fresh stream of hot water. She dropped her head back, reclining against the tub again and closed her eyes, basking in the added warmth.

It was just the barest hint of cool air. A booted heel scraped against the floor. Rachel's eyes flew open, and she jumped, water sloshing over the tub.

Anthony.

Scrambling upright, her heart skipped a beat, as she tried to arrive at a position of modesty, clasping her arms tight around her legs to hide her nudity. She tapped the pipe to stop the pumping from below to stop the overflow. "I locked the door."

"I'm a scientist. Don't you think I could pick a locked door? Clever mechanism," he praised, although he wasn't studying the tub as much as he was studying her.

He moved around the tub, his eyes staring down on her from his towering height. Regardless of the soap clouded water, could he see the flesh that shivered just beneath the surface? The notion sent bolts of heat and mortification through her.

"Clever, your use of hydraulics in the ship's pump to send the water up to the second floor."

"I left express orders that you were not to see my work until it was completed."

"But the device is complete and looking very well."

She narrowed her eyes with his double entendre. "Out! I'm indecent."

He ran his long-tapered fingers along the edge of the tub. "And leave an exciting innovation without examination? Wouldn't think of it."

She sank deeper into the water, her rapid breaths creating ripples in the water. "You are being provocative."

"Provocative is not helping me in my laboratory. Provocative is usurping my blacksmith."

So, it was to be a contest of wills. He would not win. Or could he? She stiffened her spine and lifted her chin. Careful. Plan a line of attack. "Blame your sister who corresponded the details of my invention. Your father," she cleared her throat for emphasis, "requested my engineering talents." A twinge of guilt followed, pitting father against son. This was war.

He still had the ever-present stubble across his face, giving him a rakish look—a battle he did win with his valet. Sunlight from the stained glass window above haloed him, casting him in an aura of gold. Even his thick ebony hair seemed bronzed as he leaned down to grip each side of the tub. His white shirt tucked into his fawn breeches, clung to powerful thighs, the corded muscles rippling beneath, in what could be considered indecent. Primitive.

He did not fit the formula of a scientist today. No. His posture, awareness, and confidence belied undertones of a man who always achieved what he wanted. She needed a maneuver to get him to leave. This was the other side of Anthony. The dangerous side of him. The side she had seen when he had made Sir Bonneville impotent, and again, when he dispatched the highwaymen. Her heart stopped in her throat. What kind of trouble would he cause her? She clenched and unclenched her hands with the set of events that put her at his mercy. Never had she felt so exposed and vulnerable.

Think. Get his mind on other things. Break his spell. "Why couldn't you have waited to learn about my invention?" she asked, proud that she kept any nervousness or weakness out of her voice.

His eyes darkened, with that single-mindedness of his she knew all too well. He was pursuing her, and that glint in his eye was the same one she had witnessed in the laboratory, breaking a large goal into bite-sized pieces. "Interesting your use of hydraulics. Force applied at one point, thrusting a fast flow to another point through a wetted perimeter."

Her mouth dropped from the innuendo and he laughed, a deep husky laugh while his gaze caressed the ripples of the water with suggestive fascination, and Rachel's temperature veered violently from chilled to overheated. She felt a sheen of dampness blossom above her lip.

Damn him. How she'd like to wipe that smirk off his face. She pinioned him with a glare, the same she used to sight an arrow. "Don't you have experiments to complete?"

He inclined his head in acknowledgment and grinned, his eyes lit with intellectual challenge. "In truth, I am taking great pleasure in an experiment of late."

She choked and drew her knees in tighter to her chest. He had called her bluff. What was worse, he seemed vexingly Cro-Magnon and infuriatingly unconcerned by the strength of her disdainful stare. She swept a wave of water over him, soaking him. "I am not part of your research."

His gaze swept over her face, then in lazy regard, up and down, a sweeping gesture. Her nostrils flared. He was not as unmoved as he wanted her to believe. She studied him beneath her lashes, and a smile escaped noting with power and pleasure his full arousal, forcefully outlined and tightly bound by his water soaked pants.

"We could discuss the density of water and soap in a solution, hypothesize on how long it would take for the soap residue to sink to the bottom and the water to clear, or are you afraid?"

"I don't fear you..." Though she couldn't deny the dangerous thrill hammering through her and the warmth that spread between her legs.

Footsteps. Someone marched from down the hall, paused at the door. Rachel inhaled. *To be discovered like this.*

Anthony grinned at her discomfiture and mouthed, '*I locked the door.*'

"I'm excited to see your invention," said Aunt Margaret from the corridor. "Is it finished?"

"Soon," Rachel croaked. The last thing she wanted was to go home in scandal. "*Out!*" she mimed with a pointed finger.

"Are you sure everything is all right?" prompted Aunt Margaret. "Do you need any assistance? I can call for help. What did you say?"

Rachel pleaded with Anthony with her eyes. No doubt, Aunt Margaret could not hear her. That meant getting out of the tub and yelling through the door before Anthony's aunt called the whole house for support.

He rubbed the stubble on his hard jaw, leaned closer until his lips were level with hers and whispered, "I need a quid pro-quo."

"What?" she darted an anxious glance to the door, but his hand had settled on her chin, drawing her face back to him.

His lips hovered over hers, his breath warm and spiced from cinnamon and coffee. "A kiss."

"That's illogical and you are never illogical."

"Sometimes it's good to be illogical." He threw her words back at her.

Rachel wanted to glance away, but couldn't. The man was like an elemental force, like the waxing of electrical fire, a force so fierce that nothing in his vicinity could turn away or remain unchanged—least of all her.

His lips touched hers, coaxing, persuading, enticing her lips to open. His hands slid down the gunnels pushing her on the back of the tub. Her stiffness relaxed and she melted into him as his tongue twisted, roused, thrust through her like a brand, searing her, having her. Breathing was impossible.

Her hands groped to his chest, firm healthy male flesh tingled beneath her fingertips. To touch him everywhere, to explore every part of him. She wet the silk of his shirt, brushing her fingers over muscle, heat, sighing.

He groaned, making her realize how very female she was. A wild sensuality stirred to life inside of her and she recognized it for the dangerous sensation it was. A wealth of hidden feelings leaped from her, blossoming, exploding.

He drew away. Flames licked at the ice in his blue eyes and an answering heat bloomed deep inside her. Low in her belly, and lower to her womb. The gap between them gave way to chill. Rachel managed to gulp in sweet air, her bosom still heaving.

"To arouse the scientific method." He snatched the soap.

She widened her eyes. What did that mean?

He nudged her arms away, placing one of her hands on each side of the tub. "Do not move." He massaged the bar over her breasts, giving distinct attention to first one then the other.

"Look," he demanded. He wanted her to see what he was doing, insisted that she see what he was doing to her body. He circled and tugged the nipple with the soap. His mouth curved indulgently and a lock of dark ebony hair fell carelessly down his forehead. Lifted and lathered and kneaded. The effect—something of a dream, blurring the lines between reality and imagination.

A crackle of energy burned through the water, the air, and she felt she would expire from suffocation. She lifted a hand to stop him.

A ragged murmur convulsed from his throat. "No." He returned her hand to the rim.

Her breasts grew heavy, weighted with need and so much more. Oh, how he used this wicked compulsion to gratify his experimentation.

Measure, formulate, test.

Her traitorous nipples glistened from the soap, hardened into tight coral points. She gasped, sensation ripping through her, coursing through her limbs before settling between clenched thighs. Her hips rose. To have him move the soap over her most intimate flesh.

Her mouth dropped open. She caught a moan before it escaped, lowered her hips.

Their gazes collided, the fires in his eyes darkened as his pupils dilated.

He knew. He knew the direction of her thoughts. The rogue. Knew she wanted him to touch her and not stop and that knowledge made her hands ball into fists.

To her disappointment, he dropped the soap, dried his hands on a towel, watching her. He took a ragged breath and adjusted his clothing.

"Turn around," she demanded, and when he pivoted, she rose, water sluicing onto the floor. She wrapped a towel around her and hurried to the door.

"I am fine, Aunt Margaret. Just a few finishing touches." No one was there. Rachel pivoted, far from being fine. "Your aunt is gone. Leave now, and don't look."

She tightened her grip on the towel. He stepped into the hall, gave her one final glance. "You make me feel like a large scraggly dog just unchained, scouring the landscape of the world and baying at the moon."

She slammed the door in his face.

Chapter 14

*R*achel tossed and turned in bed, finally rose, went to the windows and pulled back the drapes. The light of a full moon spilled across the floor. Burdensome clouds, clambered over each other in their haste to pass the mountain, herded by the wind and jarred like disordered concentric circles.

She fiddled with the edge of the hangings, drawing the silky fringe through her fingers. Part of her wanted to fetch Anthony to her side. But a bigger part of her was terrified and rooted her to the spot. She paced, walking in the quadrangle of moonlight. Closing her eyes, she tried to picture herself with Anthony. Hidden away in his laboratory, laying on his cot, propped up on a pillow, watching him take notes. And then he would turn and smile, gazing at her with that same smoldering sensuality that caused her insides to melt.

Oh, to have Anthony…but the fault in their destiny was the inability to see that the world falls in love with fantasy. She shook her head. No longer would she succumb to mythical notions.

She looked at her solitary bed. Since sleep had abandoned her, she might as well do something. A good book, perhaps. She threw on her robe and lit a candle, only the soft pad of her feet on the carpeted stairs echoed in the friendless quiet. In the library, she lifted her candle, illuminating row upon row of volumes marching across the shelves. She ran her fingers down numerous spines, awed of her noiseless companions and the learning to be had between the leathery jackets. At random, she selected a tome, set her candle on a table and sat on a settee, pulling her feet up beneath the folds of her robe.

Kama Sutra. Of all the books available, she had chosen the ancient Indian book of love. Authored by Vatsyayana in eighth century India and first printed on palm blocks, the book had later been illustrated and printed in Sanskrit.

Her brother and cousin had laughed and drank over the book one night when they thought she was asleep. When they were snoring in their cups, she had tip-toed into their room to sneak a peek. Jacob had awakened, slammed the book shut before her widening eyes. She'd received a strong chastisement. Yet, she possessed a curious fascination for the book that disappeared and had searched every square inch of the house.

The corners of her lips turned up. She looked over her shoulder. *Good.* The doors were shut. Everyone asleep. Unimpeded, she commenced to thumb through the forbidden pages. With certainty, she didn't understand Sanskrit. Oh my, how was it possible to achieve the suggestive physical acts between a man and a woman? She angled her head, studying the various poses. The bed in Anthony's laboratory evoked the most sinful and debauched renderings her thoughts could devise. She let out a small gasp and clutched her bosom, her hand brushing against nipples that peaked through the silk of her gown. Her breath came out in short bursts. Belly-low, her muscles tightened and her legs clamped together. Two scorching blue eyes taunted her as she relived the sweet agony of what Anthony had done to her in the bathing chamber…his lips, hot and hungry against her mouth, his desire raw and consuming, bringing forth some kind of hidden awareness interred in her from birth. All she could think—all she could think of at all—was that it could not happen.

Yet she was mesmerized with the possibilities, her mind consumed with the erotic positions the couples in the book were doing. How would it feel to lay with Anthony? To taste the hot salt of his skin, her fingers twining in the soft silk of his hair, to sample all the sensual things between a man and a woman.

She rubbed the corner of the book, flipping the pages. Logic and feelings had nothing whatsoever to do with each other.

If there was one thing she wanted, it was to lay with him before she returned home in a couple of weeks. Before she returned to the hurt and disappointment of men, rejecting her because of something out of her control. Conjuring images, the scent of sandalwood wafted over her, warm breath purred on her neck, too real. She turned. Anthony. She gasped out a small "Oh… Heat rose from the bottom of her toes to the roots of her hair.

He angled his head to the provocative pose in the Kama Sutra. How wicked was his smile? "Interesting reading."

She clapped the book shut. "I-I could not sleep."

"The text would give me insomnia."

What was she to say?

He circled the couch and sat next to her. The room fell silent, their gazes locked and the tension in the air palpable. "I had a very restless day and night, thinking *only* of you."

"Of me?"

"I want to be with you in every way a man is with a woman." He gazed at her upturned face with sensual regard, and let out a breath. "It is the time for secrets."

"Secrets?"

He stared at his folded hands in front of him. "If I tell you my secret, do you promise not to be critical."

Rachel sensed the great magnitude he wanted to share. What could have affected him so? Why would he fear her criticism? Had he committed a crime? She smoothed his queue behind his collar. "Never would I condemn you."

He tugged at his cuff.

What kernel of his life dragged him down? Her throat ached for the gifted man whose pride bound him with chains of suffocation.

"I have never been with a woman—completely."

That was all. She smiled inwardly, happy he wasn't an ax murderer. Of course, she understood his humiliation. "But you were married."

"Celeste was young, panicky, so I gave her time. When I did try to make advances she laughed at me, called me a bumbling fool. I didn't know what I was doing wrong."

Her heart skidded. Anthony existed in a prison of his own self-doubt fueled by a heartless woman. How she would like to slap Celeste.

"I was on the cusp of discovery, spending night and day in my laboratory, and then I identified my notes had been stolen."

Rachel nodded, conceding to the logic.

"Needless to say, I can't get you out of my mind and it is driving me mad. More than anything I want to be with you, like an equation—two attracted individuals proportional to the product of their affections and inversely proportional to the square of the separation between the two."

Rachel let out a breath as the spell he wove around her heightened.

"In other words, I want your body pressed against my heart, and your hands spreading my thoughts, enduring the curves of my passions and harnessing my hopes."

He wanted her.

"Oh, Anthony, the way you made me feel in the tub…"

Anthony placed a gentle finger beneath her chin and she vibrated with the nervous energy of a doe ready to leap through the forest thicket. "So we both start on even ground. Can you imagine what there is to discover?"

"Yes," she agreed, enjoying the familiarity of his touch. She trusted Anthony.

"You understand that everything I do is designed to eliminate randomness and eradicate chance. To deduce every possibility, predict every response, and mold experimentation toward a desired outcome."

The intensity of his regard pinned her to the sofa, and then the tension in his coiled muscles, the pulse throbbing at a vein in his strong neck.

"I understand your fears, Rachel."

She dragged her palms across her skirts. He referred to her near defilement.

"There is a bottom of society that has evil intent...that wants power over another human being. That is not the relationship between a man and a woman. The person who attacked you should be hanged. I would kill anyone who tried to harm you. I treasure you, Rachel, honor and adore you. At any time, you want me to stop, I will. If you want to cry, we can hold hands."

Tears gathered in her eyes, grateful for his patience and compassion. Sunshine and hope, rising out of the world of shadows and pain. His large hand took her face and held it gently, his thumb brushing the wetness away, his touch almost unbearable in its tenderness. His hands slipped into her hair and brought her closer.

There was nothing more that Anthony desired to do but kiss her. He waited for her to bolt, would understand immediately—he intuitively knew her thoughts.

The candle sputtered then breathed its last, leaving them in a swath of blazing moonlight. He felt her yielding and then restrained himself, for he needed to keep his head. Yet images of her in the bathing chamber and her reaction that afternoon exploded, the discovery of what she was reading, and now, the transparent silk of her gown and what lay beneath wreaked havoc with his senses. She was his, always would be, and he liked that fact. His body heated like electrical fire as her soft curves melted into him. He pushed back her robe, and hungrily his mouth covered hers, his tongue tracing the contours.

"You've defined the question, Anthony. Shouldn't we begin to test hypothetical explanations through observation and measurement of the subject?"

She wanted him.

Her hands slid up his arms and linked about his neck, her fingers winding in the tendrils of his hair in the back of his neck. Aroused now, his one hand lowered to the small of her back while his lips moved down her throat, following the elegant curve to the collarbone, right where the edge of her gown met skin. He nudged it down, tasting one new inch of her, exploring the soft, salty sweetness, and shuddering with pleasure when he cupped the rounded swell of her breast with his hand, feeling her nipple firm under his touch.

"I do not want to frighten you." He kissed her, reached down and brought up the silk of her gown, feeling the long satiny smoothness of her knee and thigh. The minute she moaned, his tongue plunged into her mouth and the kiss exploded. His hand cupped the soft flesh of her bottom and pulling her against him, making her aware of his aroused body. She stiffened at the forced intimacy, and then pressed her soft body into him.

"I have no idea what I'm doing," he rasped.

"Don't stop."

She was driving him insane with need. He tasted the honeyed sweetness of her lips, mingling with the wine he drank, and then buried his face in the valley of her breasts. She pushed his hand to the bare flesh between her thighs, and moaned when he found the hot, wet heat of her and slipped two fingers inside.

Kama Sutra had laid a steady roadmap. Part one fitted in part two. Damn. His body ached with the need for release, for the ease he knew he could find inside her. He suckled her breast and moved his fingers in and out, analyzed and memorized her reactions. He touched her center. She bucked. Interesting. To experience the hot heady perfume of her feminine arousal.

"Anthony. Too much."

Tentatively, she smoothed her hand over his erection bound by his breeches. He yanked her hand away. Afraid he had no control.

Her swollen lips pouted. "I need to experiment." She resumed her stroking.

His mouth swooped down on hers. He ground into her hand. Blood rushed to his groin. His gut clenched tight. No control. He shuddered. *Exploded.*

In a span of a second, she tore her mouth from his, demanding desperately that he stop, whispering frantically to him. She shoved him away, just as a rustling sound penetrated his senses. He angled his head to the noise. Blinked.

Aunt Margaret.

He pulled her gown down and stood, closing his coat over the stain in his breeches. He stepped between Rachel and Aunt Margaret, presenting a shield, so Rachel would have time to right herself. They had been in the shadows of the sofa. He was certain his maidenly aunt had not seen or heard anything as she entered. How convenient her timing. She possessed the same targeting as a homing pigeon. A growl erupted from his throat. "It is late, Aunt Margaret."

She held her candle up to light his face, her ever-present ear horn drooping from her neck. She must sleep with the item.

"What a ferocious scowl, Anthony. Why you look like a bear deprived of its dinner. Why is that?" She didn't wait for an answer but toddled over to a table, lit a candle from hers. She inspected the shelves, taking her time, selecting a book.

"I'm having trouble sleeping," she said over her shoulder.

Anthony doubted that notion.

She returned, craning her head around him. "There you are, Miss Thorne. Are you looking for a book, too? Are you having trouble sleeping?"

"The physiology of cats?" Anthony inclined his head to his Aunt' choice of books.

She raised her ear horn to her ear.

"You hate cats," he shouted.

Aunt Margaret dropped her ear horn and waved a hand in airy dismissal. "I've taken a sudden interest in them. Well off I go to bed. We have a busy day in the lab tomorrow. You two go to bed, too," she said.

Anthony did a double take at her suggestion. "If you say so." Just short of murder, his mind burned with ways to get rid of his wandering, unfortunate aunt who seemed to show up at precisely the wrong time. A new bacteria? Virus?

Rachel exhaled behind him. "Do you think—"

Anthony's lips twisted into a cynical smile, the force of his voice unleashed his great annoyance. "No, she did not see anything."

"Thank you." Relief mirrored in her face. "I could not bear another scandal."

She took his hand, the soft pad of her thumb, smoothing across his knuckles. "Could we just sit?"

Just sit? He let loose a breath of frustration. Dampness seeping through his breeches, he grimaced at his lack of control. He needed to change.

The gentle touch of her fingers, and the look in her eyes cemented his resolve. Anthony moved her to the settee, sheltering her in his arms, content with the wild beating of her heart upon his chest.

He rubbed the back of his neck. "I apologize for—"

"You made me feel wonderful."

His chest expanded, gratitude for this astonishing woman who saw past his humiliation and rewarded him with her generous spirit. He pulled her closer, thinking about her resilience. Strong and bending like a willow in the wind. That her life had been chaotic, that she had suffered agonies which would have stripped a normal soul of its sanity, and then, faced the torment of isolation. And yet, all the darkness of the world could not extinguish her dazzling light.

Without a doubt, she flouted rules of convention with her brilliance. She peppered comments with sarcasm, adapting an air of fearlessness, in which people were drawn by her charisma and charm, but beneath the bolstered air of confidence hid a woman who was unable to show her vulnerability to others—except to him.

Anthony enumerated her assets. How she made light of a situation to defuse tension. Her instinctual sense of people—Lord Ward, Captain Johnson, Joseph Banks. Her insatiable curiosity in the workings of science, her amusement and amazement even in the smallest things like birds that flew through the forests and the frost scintillating in the winter air. Wasn't she the antithesis of his predictability? Didn't she stand up to his ire, encouraging him, divining her confidence and determination, knowing he'd succeed? Didn't she match his own work ethic and gratification in achievement? Wasn't she sympathetic, an attentive listener, cheering him on no matter how small his successes were? Most endearing was her wry sense of humor, no matter the predicament. She made him laugh at life, pulling him from his dark grimness to her light.

Then there was her compassionate and responsible nature, caring for her younger brother, administrating a shipyard and all its workers. How she treated people with kindness, right down to the idiotic blacksmith and his meddling aunt. With Rachel, he opened his eyes to the good in humanity and the world. She was his life rope.

He nuzzled the top of her head, inhaling lavender and lemon balm, her scent, experiencing the most extraordinary torment. He reclined stiffly as she stroked his chest, then grabbed her hand to end her simple exploration before something started that he would not be able to rein in.

Her eyelashes swept down upon her cheeks, long and sooty and he watched the rise and fall of her breasts, warm, full, enticing. So, while the stars played in the skies, Anthony contented himself until she fell asleep, and then carried her upstairs. She sighed then, and nestled her face into his chest before he laid her on the bed. Glancing down upon her silken head, her chestnut hair, gleaming in the meager light and fanned across the pillow in splendor, brought warmth to his heart.

"Anthony," she murmured and stuck her hand out searchingly. He pulled a deep breath. He was the last thought on her mind. How he would like to crawl into bed with her. The whole world could be damned. She was his and he made up his mind to court her. He closed the door to her room and shook his head.

All I wanted was a husband and children.

He'd give her all her dreams on a silver platter.

Chapter 15

*B*athed a hundred times, brushed, combed and clipped, Rachel's stray had been cleared of lice, and the two open sores on the legs had healed. Boasting a high glossy brown and white feathered coat, and with doe-like eyes, and a docked tail, wagging to show its pleasure, the dog presented an irresistible companion. Easy to train and loyal to the end, she slept on the floor next to Rachel's bed. Now with the dog trotting at her heels, Rachel burst through the door of the laboratory.

"You're late," Anthony announced, eyes narrowed. "I'm allergic to dogs."

The dog circled twice, flopping on the bed Rachel had made beneath the window—despite Anthony's protestations. "You've told me a million times. And you are not allergic. You haven't sneezed once in the past five days."

"I walk twenty feet away and can still smell the dog. And how did you get my father wrapped around your finger? Never did I believe he'd allow that beast in the house. It belongs in the kennels."

Rachel lifted her nose in the air. "Your father says she will be an excellent guard dog."

"I noted when she ran off while we were attacked by the highwaymen. The mutt doesn't even have a name yet."

Rachel tossed her hair behind her shoulder. "She was kicked by a bull of a man if you remember. And I've decided to name her Caia Caecilia, calling her Casey for short, because she likes to sleep next to the hearth."

"After the Roman Goddess of Fire? Why not, Dimwit, a name she can live up to?"

Rachel rubbed Casey behind the ears, reassuring the animal. "You are being provocative. Your father says she is a champion and very intelligent." To demonstrate, Rachel rolled a bottle across the floor. The dog tore across the slippery tiles, sliding and snatching the bottle in her dazzling white teeth.

"Let it retrieve bones like a normal dog."

His disapproval pierced her with the precision of an archer's arrow. Rachel straightened. Anthony's real frustration was on the negative results of his experiments. Wasn't it? She felt herself heat from her toes to the roots of her hair, remembering the way he had touched her in the library and a million times since, finding excuses to steal kisses from her, his breath hot on her ear as he nibbled her lobe. How he shuddered when she ran her hands over his broad shoulders and muscular chest. If he touched her now, she feared she would incinerate, and if he didn't, she'd die.

"Casey likes bottles." Rachel threw a sock doll across the floor to demonstrate. The dog ignored it. Then she rolled a bottle. "Attack."

The dog attached her teeth to the bottle and shook her head with a ferocious growl.

"Useful. Think of all the butterflies and sparrows the beast will take down."

"You are too cynical and need to be less critical. This dog will protect us."

"That's after she runs off after an imaginary squirrel."

The dog let go of the bottle at Anthony's feet, dropped to the floor, resting her head on her front paws, and blinked.

With a grudge, he patted the dog. Rachel smiled. Wars were won by inches.

She hung up her coat, tied on an apron, and turned, caught Anthony staring at her with rabid intensity, just as he had at the ball when she was wearing her emerald silk, freezing her into place and melting her all at once. *Kama Sutra.* Oh, my. Was he thinking of those sensual images, too? A crackle of energy passed between them, hot and raw and carnal. With certainty, he had those erotic images branded on his mind.

Oh, the things he did to her without final consummation, watching her, touching her, kissing her in her most intimate places. To have to bite down on her lip, to muffle her screams. How was it possible? And didn't she experiment with him too? Delightful, wicked torments, to experience the delicious power she had over him.

Impossible to stop the constant state of arousal she was in next to him. To sweep the bottles off the counter and demand he take her now. She cleared her throat and looked away.

A huge bouquet of flowers was set beneath the clock. She inhaled the exotic scents. Lilies, orchids, and bird-of-paradise delivered from the conservatory. A new bouquet greeted her every day since the night in the library. Her stomach fluttered. Anthony was a romantic.

But this was business now and they had experiments to perform before she returned to Boston, only days away. Her heart dipped at the thought and she shook it aside. "What are we working on today?"

Following Anthony's instructions, Rachel soaked flannel discs in an acid solution. She compressed her lips, trying to concentrate. Anthony had conceded to her idea. "Each metal has a certain power, which is different from metal to metal, of setting the electrical fluid to motion."

"You are so unlike the young women I know."

"Really? Do tell." Was he courting her? Hadn't he accepted the dog, brought her flowers from the conservatory, gone on walks when she requested the exercise? Hadn't he been by her side, attending balls and dinners in between working in the lab? *Unpredictable.*

He frowned. "We have work to do, and I'm not about to rain down further compliments on a head that is already full of confidence."

"How disappointing. Where is Aunt Margaret?"

"She was feeling under the weather and bid us good luck on our experiments." He took out the metal discs, the copper flashing a bright orange in the light. "I like the way you roll up your sleeves and get things done, taking pride in your work. Efficient."

She twisted a lock of her hair. *A compliment?* "Go on."

His notebook lay open. Drawn in the margin was a heart with Rachel and Anthony stenciled inside. Her toes curled. She would rip out that page and carry it home with her to treasure forever.

Anthony stacked the copper and zinc discs, tonging the acid drenched flannel between. "You are the antidote to my severe, demanding, pigheadedness. I like your observations and most important, your witty comebacks. You make me laugh."

Regrets. The people she'd miss, Aunt Margaret, the Duke, Sebastian, the butler and *Anthony.* Her throat thickened. They had been more than family. *Think forward to Abby, Jacob, Ethan and the baby. Leave. Don't' think about it, don't look back.*

But to whirl in a circle, to sample Anthony's attention, this indulgence—even for a short time? When she walked by, she heard him inhale her hair. "I really feel we are on the brink of something that will change all mankind. Have you thought of the possibilities?" she said.

He didn't say anything, his shoulder muscles tightened, intent on finishing the stack. Rachel clutched her chest. *One two three.* Attached to the top and bottom of the pile, Anthony joined the two wires. A small charge emitted. Her shoulders sank. The experiment failed.

Anthony raked his fingers through his hair. "I told you it wouldn't work."

"It did work. We ruled out a possibility. What do *you* propose next?" She refused to let him sink to despair, the same despondency she drowned in every day, knowing she would be saying goodbye.

"It's useless. Day after day, we try repeatedly, harvesting nothing."

She scuffed a chair closer to the cabinet and looked him right in the eye. "One of the older and wiser carpenters in the Thorne Shipyard used to tell me theories are like stars. You never really succeed in touching them with your fingers, but like the ancient seafaring men on the desert of waters, used them as their guides and discovered their path."

"Platitudes," Anthony groaned. "No matter how small my successes you always cheer me on. Let's stack a higher pile."

"That's my Anthony, back on his problem solving. Oh, the perils of being a genius." She wagged a finger at him. "Have you ever experienced the threat of humility?"

He offered her a hopeless grin.

"Well, wisdom is knowing what to do next. Let's try mixing a salt and acid solution."

"Interesting." He compromised and dumped the existing solution to start over again. Rachel joined him at the sink, pumping water and washing the jars, and when the task was completed carried the equipment to the counter and started the process again. Anthony poured the sulfuric acid and Rachel measured in a salt brine solution, soaking new flannel discs.

Copper, flannel, zinc, were alternated and supported by three glass rods. Anthony picked up the two wires, glanced at her. "Let's hope."

She clapped her hands together in a prayerful pose. *Please. Please. Let it work this time.*

He connected the two ends and she held her breath.

Electrical fire zinged around the room like shooting stars, hurling against the walls of the laboratory. The dog barked and leaped.

Rachel had almost forgotten to breathe, for her entire body steeped with the most powerful and intense sensation she'd ever known. It was something like frenzied hunger, and something like fulfillment. It was wonder and awe and yearning and fear captured in a bold new world. Her chest expanded with it until pressed against her lungs, emptying them of breath. There were no words other than to have Anthony at her side and sit on the edge of the heavens at the dawn of creation.

She threw her hands into the air and cried out. "Oh, Anthony, you are magnificent. Do you realize what you have discovered?"

"We," he emphasized and she loved the ring of that, "We have discovered the first method for the generation of a sustained electrical current, and creating a high energy source."

He reached out one long arm reached out and caught her to him, like a lion interrupting the pulsing rush of an eagle. "If you don't want me to fall in love with you, you're going to have to start not looking so lovely. Maybe have the seamstress sew a couple of potato sacks together."

She widened her eyes.

"I'm not jesting. You're too beautiful."

He pushed her back until she bumped against the cabinet. His mouth skimmed her jaw, down her throat, his teeth grazing her skin and the shadow of his beard scratching her.

Before I go...

She pushed at him, holding his hands. A part of her told her that she should stop, that she should think this through, but the other voices in her head drowned her out. She wanted him more than she wanted to breathe.

"I want to be with you."

Tension in the air snapped like the rigging on a full-blown sail. "You know this is illogical," he said.

"Sometimes it is good to be illogical."

Chapter 16

*R*achel gasped when he gathered her into his arms and carried her to the other room, shutting the door with his foot, a latch clicked into place. He stood her beside the cot. "What we are to do, Rachel is between a man and woman, *husband and wife.*"

She pressed two fingers to his lips. "I want this to be magic, to be memorable."

"Do not move," he ordered.

With no opposition from her, he reached behind and unfastened a row of buttons, pushing away her dress. She shivered as the delicate gown glided down her body and pooled at her feet. He tugged at her lacings, tossed the corset away. Naked now, Rachel covered herself. He moved her hands to her sides, her nipples grazing the soft silk of his shirt.

"You never need to cover yourself. You are beyond beautiful."

Trapped in a whirl of heady arousal, she watched, intrigued as he shirked out of his shirt, reveling in the lean muscularity of his chest, arms and shoulders. She longed to run her hands across his skin, to glide her fingers over every muscle and sinew of him. Her gaze followed the line of hair rising from beneath his breeches to his chest, admiring his trim waist and the width of his shoulders. Pulsing heat spread between her legs.

"What if someone discovers us?"

He looked over his shoulder. "The lock would hold back an invasion of the Huns."

Rachel moistened her lips with the tip of her tongue. He watched her with hunger in his eyes. A slight sheen lit his body, sleek, and strong, without the excess bulk conspicuous of nobility. He finished shedding his breeches, and her eyes widened, her gaze riveted to his manhood, impressive and frightening.

"I will be gentle with you," he promised.

Husband and wife. A proposal? Her heart hammered. *Impossible.* But his tenderness was her undoing, for she grew terrified and excited and she wanted it to be him before she withdrew to the isolation of Boston as a lonely spinster. To have this experience with the man she loved but could not have.

"This is a time for sharing, a time for loving." Reverently, he lay her on the bed, and then took her in his arms, pillowing his head in the veil of her hair. He smelled wonderful. Clean, strong, vital male. They gazed into each other's eyes awed by the majesty of the moment, both understanding and yearning for so much more.

He brushed her hair with his fingertips. "How many times have I conjured this very moment in my mind? Now you are here in my arms, your warmth and sweet scent to taunt me."

With incredible perceptiveness, she sensed his vulnerability and reached up to stroke his cheek, outlining the sharp-angled planes of his face. She memorized everything about him. To know the way his analytical mind worked, his fight and thrill of discovery, his persistence, and talent. The way he kept her safe and secure. The way he listened to the wrongs inflicted on her. His consideration, his caring, his gaze riveted on her with tenderness. There existed a million different things about him that she held to her heart.

"Let this time be a long series of experiments," she whispered. She was a trembling bow-string ready to snap.

Rachel felt the hard boldness of him, pressed to her side, saw the smoldering flames in his eyes. He bent to take her lips, searing a trail down her throat and shoulder. A warm hand closed over her breast, caressing in circles then capturing a nipple and squeezing it between his fingers before trailing to her next breast. She reached up and smoothed her hands over his shoulder, feeling his heat like a hot iron beneath her fingertips.

He crushed her to him, his hands exploring the hollows of her back and down over her hips, automatically she curled into the curve of his body. Her breasts tingled against the muscles of his chest. His hand and lips were everywhere, the gentle massage sending currents of desire through her. His mouth moved to her breast, his tongue caressed her sensitive swollen nipple.

"Do you like that?"

"Yes." She arched toward him.

His hand seared a path down her abdomen and onto her thigh. He stroked there and she groaned, pushing her hips into his hand. His palm sought the warmth of her woman's mound, circling her wet cleft. She jerked.

"Fascinating." He did it again. She writhed.

Urging her thighs further apart, he slid his fingers deep into her.

Heat scorched her belly and lower, a distinct warmth flooded between her legs. She whimpered unable to get enough, raising her hips to the splendid mastery of his fingers, sinking and withdrawing.

"I must test and retest," he said raggedly.

He kissed her with raw passion, parting her lips, and setting her nerves ablaze with a slow search for her tongue. Rachel's hands crept around his neck, her breath labored, her body turning light and hot. When he dragged his mouth from hers, she kept her arms around him, her head spinning.

"I want to ask you a very pointed but hypothetical question."

"What's your question?" she said unsteadily.

"I don't want you to go back to America."

"That's a statement, not a question." Oh, why did he stop now? She swallowed and found the courage to look up at him. "Your wife should be of nobility and of equivalent pedigree."

"We will discuss this later."

"Anthony?"

"Hmm?" His lips played at the sensitive corners of her mouth. She had one week remaining. "I'm leaving."

"And I'm allergic to dogs."

Like a bird in a cage that sings when it knows it is dying, she said, "I cannot fill those shoes especially if you are to be the next duke. I have to go."

"We'll see about your departure."

"You cannot stop me."

"Hush," he cradled her face in his hands. Brushed his lips over hers. "I'll make sure it doesn't happen even if I have to chain you to this lab." His fingertips slid up and down her slender neck, toying with the fine curls at her nape. He nudged her legs apart, continued his stroking until she cried out for that intangible, elusive sensation to give her release. He withdrew his hand, pushing her thighs apart. "Look at me," he said fiercely, staring into her face.

Her dark lashes lifted, and she held his intense gaze. She grabbed him then, guided him to her. He thrust slowly into her with incredible control, and then stopped.

"From what I've heard, it will hurt for only, a moment."

He looked so severe and concerned above her. With trembling fingers, she touched his jaw. "I trust you."

He drove into her and muffled her cry with his smoldering kisses. He stopped. "I'm so sorry, Rachel."

She moved, adjusting to his throbbing fullness. He began anew. Each time, he penetrated a little further, stretching her, moving with insistent rhythm. Rachel stroked the smooth surface of his back, and her pleasure mounted. Her fingers dug into the plane of his muscle. His breath faster now. Her fingers drifted from his shoulders, digging into his hips, her heart racing. She heard him whisper to her then, in broken phrases he couldn't seem to hold back. "You're beautiful...so intelligent...*I love you.*"

Confused, disbelieving, silken desire exploded within her, around her like the electrical fire that bounced off the walls, ceiling and floor. She was drowning in feelings she could not name or describe as his hands clenched her buttocks now, lifted her, felt him suck in his breath, stiffen and then plunge into her, waves of warmth poured from him.

They lay entwined as lovers, drifting off to sleep, and then making love again...and again. The musk and scent of his body filled her nostrils and she was floating in languid contentment. It was all a dream, a wonderful fairytale, and yet, she had to give it all up.

That it was done of her love for him yielded the greatest sacrifice of all.

She would take home memories that time would never erase, but the heartbreaking reality was knowing that an eternity would not make the soul-drenching loss forgettable. Only bearable.

In the gossamer haze of the late afternoon, sunlight stretched long shadows, glistening on the glassware, shimmering over the cabinets and gliding over the cot in a subdued riot of color. Still joined intimately to her, Anthony stirred, a frown marring his handsome face. "Perhaps we can come home early from that dratted ball you need to attend and discuss the universe."

She bit her lip. Next week she'd sail to Lisbon, and then home. Whatever time she had remaining she would share with Anthony. "We could arrive late. Could draw some more conclusions."

"Agreed. I'm on the precipice of something more and not accustomed to finalizing conclusions after only five observations."

With heavy-lidded eyes, she stretched cat-like, loving the feel of him already hardening in her. "Better make it six observations—to be sure."

She was like warm pliant clay, her body damp with perspiration, her arms limp on the pillow. Anthony rolled and cradled her in his arms. Rachel smoothed a finger over Anthony's chest. "I can delay no longer. I need to go and dress before someone comes looking for us."

Casey barked. The dog ran back and forth to the cot.

"What is wrong with the dog?"

Anthony nuzzled her. "Probably can't get to my favorite flask."

She pushed at his chest. "The ruff is up on her collar. What if it is a servant who has come to remind us to get ready for the evening's event?"

Anthony cursed and heaved himself from the bed, jerked on his pants and shirt, pattered out into the laboratory. "No one is here."

Rachel breathed a sigh of relief, dressed, then presented her back to Anthony, allowing him to fasten her buttons.

"I rather like this domestic responsibility." He placed her coat about her shoulders, and then kissed her long and lingeringly. "You go on ahead and get ready for the evening's event. I'll clean up the lab."

Chapter 17

*A*nthony sprinted to the house. How much more entranced could he be? He had begun to imagine the magic that he could feel, and if he feared of anything, it was that he might never come to a place in his life again when he could know such sweet and soaring pleasure. Night cloaked the firmament and an amethyst strip lay across the sky, studded with stars. Despite her ridiculous protestations, Rachel would be his wife, sleeping next to him, and they would watch the sun come up over the horizon and spread across the estate. As duke, he could marry anyone he desired. To hell with tradition.

She was his, destined from the beginning of time, and there lay a certain male pride in that fact. He couldn't wait for the vows, but deep down, she was already his in every word and deed. All their barriers had faded away, and for the first time in his life, he was filled with a tenderness so deep he ached inside.

He could love.

That Rachel could teach him to love was without a doubt the enchantment she spun and he was caught forever in her web. He even looked forward to the ball this evening, hosted by the Duke of Banfield. No doubt Rachel was ready and waiting for him. He ducked his head in the library. Not there. Caught Sebastian in the hall. "Is Rachel ready?"

"I did not see her come back from the laboratory."

Perfect reasoning suggested she was dressing. Anthony sprinted up the stairs, cornered Mrs. Noot carrying mending from Rachel's room. "Have you see Miss Thorne?

Mrs. Noot shrugged. "I haven't seen her since morn. I've been waiting for her."

The hackles raised on his neck. He raced down the stairs. Broke into a run. His father shouted. Outside, his foot slipped on an iced flagstone, and righted himself. The pause allowed him to hear a whimper in the rear of the bushes. Two guards lay bound. A lump the size of a hen's egg bulged on the side of one of the guard's head. An envelope was pinned to his coat.

"Where is she?"

"Got hit from behind."

His heart dropped to the pit of his stomach. The great danger Rachel found herself in was a result of his negligence. No chance the scoundrel was still around. He would have left as soon as he had her. Was she still alive? Of course. His unseen enemy wanted the Rutland heir. Hands shaking, Anthony tore open the envelope. A muscle jumped in his jaw.

He tore inside the house. His father stepped from the bottom of the stairs. Ten staff members assembled. Sebastian raised a brow. More guards came in from behind him. Anthony waved the letter. "I must trade myself for Rachel."

Anthony's stallion whickered in the woods where he tied him several yards back from Captain Elijah Johnson's house. Nose down, the dog prowled beside him, growling. Right place. Casey smelled Rachel. "Stay." The dog froze on the spot, whining. Not at all happy of being left behind.

"I'll get her back."

Anthony had told his father and the guards to come ten minutes later. To hold back, so he could arbitrate and get Rachel out alive.

He pressed an ear to the crack of the door to the old sea captain's house. No sound. Not good. They were waiting for him. How many? He eased open the door and slipped inside, moving across planked floors that moaned with age. A half-moon cast long eerie shadows across water stained walls, illuminating the interior as bright as day. Clutter and debris stacked everywhere, the peculiar trait of a hoarder. An ongoing battle between rat feces and mold rioted the air. Broken furniture had been used for firewood. Rinds of smoky bacon greased the floor. He nudged the ashes in the fireplace with the toe of his boot, the embers still warm...someone lived here of late.

He heard the click of a flint-lock pistol before a massive blow slammed against the side of his skull, making him see stars.

Groggy, Anthony moved his head sending a jolt of pain through his skull. He flexed his hand to locate the source, but he couldn't move. It was as if he was paralyzed. But, as his vision cleared, he saw, he sat in a chair with numerous coils wrapped tightly around him. He closed his eyes, trying to remember. Nothing. A total blank. *Think.* Still nothing. Only darkness.

"Are you awake, Anthony?"

Rachel. His heart soared.

"I'm tied on a chair right behind you."

He groaned. "Where we are?

The scrape of boots on a stairway and a lantern held high, scattered light, diminishing the shadows. "Greetings, Lord Anthony. Welcome to your final resting place, the attic of the late Captain Johnson."

He shook his head to clear the haze. "Cuthbert Noot?"

"Of course."

"I see you are hale and healthy, back from the dead." Gone was the former well-groomed estate manager. Filthy, missing teeth, ragged clothing, that coal-dust speech. "Except for your exceptional wart, you've changed your appearance, Cuthbert."

Cuthbert grinned like a Gargoyle. Unhinged. "No thanks to you, Lord Anthony. I survived the prison. A friend helped me. I'm going to kill the both of you, then the rest of your family."

"My assistant, George? The flowerpot? The axle on the carriage? I assume your maneuverings?" Anthony spat out, his words spiked with venom. He hated the bastard for catching him unaware. "The deal was to trade Miss Thorne for me."

"No deal."

Anthony cursed his own stupidity in not keeping more of a vigilant eye and the prey of such a beast as Cuthbert Noot. Wished he had made his father's timeline to five minutes. To keep Cuthbert talking was imperative. "Who helped you? Had to be someone with influence?"

Cuthbert laughed so hard, he choked on his saliva. "I'll take that secret to my grave. He's rich and powerful. Got me out of Newgate, staged a fight where another inmate was killed to take my place. All's I had to do was agree to kill you. Like getting ten Christmases wrapped in one neat package."

Rachel's dog howled outside.

"Who else is helping you? You must have had help, getting my assistant's body to Lord Chelmsford's."

"I have four of my men downstairs. Newgate recruits eager for a coin."

Blood dripped from Anthony's head wound, down his forearm and pooled on the floor as he strained against the the ropes. Cuthbert was good at knots. "Four? You'll need more than that."

"Brave words, Lord Anthony. You'll never get free." Cuthbert's lips pulled back. "Percy Devol may have failed and your sister lucked out—for the time being. Heard she had a brat. He'll die with her husband."

Rachel seethed behind him. "Jacob will kill anyone who comes close to his wife and child."

"What do you plan to do with us?" Anthony asked the inevitable, listening to the dog ratchet up its barking. He felt Rachel's fingers, trying to undo the knots. An exercise in futility.

Cuthbert fixed him with a disquieting intense stare. "I plan a slow death. Fire. My men are moving wood into the living room, building a roaring fire. A drawn-out death for you and Miss Thorne, Lord Anthony, like you planned for me in Newgate."

His heart sank. The house was a pile of tinder. Once the inferno started there would be no escape. "Let Miss Thorne go."

"You think I'm mad? There will be no witnesses."

"You won't get away with it. There will be investigations."

"And like the other investigations your father has started, nothing will come of it. That rich lordship will make sure of it like he did the others."

Cuthbert's eyes were dead, devoid of any humanity, the opaque grey darting over Rachel exhibited an unnatural pagan gleam. "Your wife cuckolded you. Had an affair with Lord Ward, planning to meet him the day she died."

"You're lying." Cuthbert's revelation hit him like a sucker punch.

"I startled her horse…it reared…she fell…knocked the breath out of her. I had my time with her. Spread her legs like the whore she was, begging and screaming."

"You, son of a bitch." Anthony's ears pounded. Celeste did not die from a random fall. She'd been murdered.

"Didn't breathe her last right away. No, I took my time. Made her do all sorts of things. His Lordship got bored, so I snapped her neck. Easy."

"You sick bastard." Despite Celeste's selfishness and infidelity, she didn't deserve to die that way. "Who is his Lordship?"

Cuthbert leaned into Anthony's face, his breath tainted with rancid bacon. "You'll never know who he is. I'm going to get that traitorous wife of mine and strangle her…and take great delight doing so. Make her pay. Maybe I'll take a time or too with the Colonial. Let you watch."

"Keep your hands off her." Anthony fought against the ropes, every muscle and sinew pushed beyond endurance. The thought of Cuthbert touching Rachel brought out his sinister impulses. *Bonneville. The highwaymen.* He had barely stopped himself from snapping their neck's in front of her.

Smoke spiraled up the stairs. Cuthbert cackled. "My men have a nice fire started. Sorry, Miss Thorne to deprive you of the pleasure of my company. I'll bid you adieu." He hung the lantern on a beam and clunked down the stairs.

"You should not feel responsible for your wife, Anthony," Rachel said. "I know the guilt you carried, not protecting her—"

What a fool he'd been. No wonder Celeste hadn't wanted him to accompany her. Brick by brick, the wall he'd spent so many years erecting and fortifying, splintered and shattered.

"Celeste had culpability cheating on you with Lord Ward. Cuthbert killed her. None of what occurred with Celeste was your fault. It was evil."

How he had distanced himself for protection, wallowing in the delusion of being unable to love. Celeste did not love him. Love went both ways.

"A wise man once told me, '*The experiences of our past are the architects of our present and to not let the bad overwhelm what is good*'."

Rachel lashed him with his own words. For the first time in eons, the gnawing ache inside him faded away.

"We've got to get free."

Rachel stated the obvious.

Anthony worked at the knots, scanning the contents of the attic. The reclusive sea captain had a collection of oddities that would have rivaled Montagu House Museum in Bloomsbury. Outside, Casey's barking echoed through the countryside. Cuthbert and his men slammed the door. Would they gloat at the fireworks?

"See that bottle on the table labeled, sulfuric acid? Do you think it's really sulfuric acid? Casey! Here Casey!" She called to the dog.

The woman was made for bedlam. "No matter how faithful you think that mutt is, she will never hurl herself into fire. And what can she do, untie knots with her teeth?"

"Casey! Here Casey!"

Nothing. Then through the snap and crackle of fire rushed the patter of paws. Hair singed, the dog jumped on Anthony, licking his face."

"You were saying?"

Anthony scoffed. "Impress me with your next feat. The mutt will sprout wings and fly?"

She cooed to the dog. "Get the bottle."

The dog ran and retrieved the bottle.

Rachel stretched her fingers, grasped the bottom of the flask.

"Unbelievable. If we get out of this alive, the mutt can have all the bottles she wants. Oceans of them. Next is the tricky part." Anthony jumped his chair closer to Rachel's, stretched his fingers, pulled the stopper out. "Pour it on the ropes, not my hands. There is rapid destruction of skin tissue if it comes in contact, goes right to the bone."

"You don't have to remind me, but you try performing the task tied to a chair."

Anthony spread his hands away, leaned forward. He smelled acid burning through jute.

"How long do you estimate?"

He heard the worry in her voice, grunted, using his weight to tug against the rope so it would snap. "Couldn't even guess?"

"That's unusual. You always have a formula."

"Did think once about how long it would take Lord Ward to dissolve in a vat of acid."

"How long?"

"Three hours to make a nice brown soup of him. That's if I added three-hundred-degree heat."

Fire crackled and exploded beneath the floorboards. "We don't have three hours. And did you have to remind me of the heat?"

All he wanted to do was take her in his arms and comfort her. The rope snapped. They both crashed to the floor. He rubbed his wrists. The dog nuzzled Anthony's face. "Good Casey." He stood, his muscles, sluggish, each of his movements like a delayed reaction. He scratched the dog behind the ears.

"Do you realize you called the dog by her real name?"

Anthony looked upon Rachel with veneration, followed her to the window. The murky silhouettes of treetops emerged in the pre-dawn light. Too far to the ground. Cuthbert leaned against a tree, glorying. No trace of his men. Anthony ground his teeth. They would get away.

"It's our only escape route," Anthony said.

Like kindling on fire, the ancient wood frame house snapped, popped and spit...a matter of time before it leapt through the floorboards. Smoke filled the room. A block and tackle beckoned, rope, yards of it...a crossbow and quiver of arrows. His mind sped with possibilities.

Move! He staggered to the block and tackle, so weak from where Cuthbert bashed him in the head. He stumbled...fell. Rachel rushed to his side, propped her arm under him and helped him lean against a post. He closed and opened his eyes to clear his vision. How would they get out of here without his help?

"I know what you're thinking." She uncoiled the ropes, helping him thread it through the block and tackle. She fashioned a looped chair to sit in, securing it with sailor's knots, slanting him a smile. "Working in a shipyard has its advantages. The sailors make these chairs to work on the side of the ship when out at sea."

On tiptoe, she stood on a chair and secured the rope to the ceiling. On a support beam a crossbow hung. She retrieved it.

"I'm thinning the rope. It is too heavy for the arrow." He tied the end of the rope with an arrow. Fire heated the floor. Anthony sweated, rose and shook his head. Better now.

She looked out the window. "Must shoot high to carry the weight."

"I estimate a forty-degree arc, considering the weight of rope, force and velocity and gravity," Anthony said.

Rachel nodded. "How good are you with a crossbow?"

"Never tried."

"I suppose that elects me to the position. Different than a bow, but I think I can manage. There are only three arrows. What I'm worried about is the arrow getting caught in the tree branches."

Locking the nut into place, she placed the nose stirrup on the floor and pulled back on both sides of the string with all her might. She picked up the crossbow, leveled it on the windowsill, loaded the arrow against the string, checked over her shoulder to make sure the rope had plenty of slack, sighted, and pulled the trigger. The arrow sailed, past the tree.

Anthony wiped the dampness from his brow with his coat sleeve and helped her retrieve the rope. "Can't give up now, my love. The trajectory is off on the crossbow. Aim more to the left."

She pushed another arrow into the crossbow and eyed down the center. "How many degrees to the left would you estimate?"

"Twenty degrees. You'll do fine," he assured her.

"Now who sounds like the optimist? Seems strange talking in navigational terms when we are navigating a crossbow and our lives depend on my aim. Forty-degrees high, twenty left. Like following a duck."

Up and to the side, she aimed and fired. An explosion from below created a wind, hurled the arrow off its trajectory and into the branches of the trees. *Damn.*

Anthony pulled and pulled on the rope, the arrow fell off.

He went rigid. A searing hot pain tore into his right forearm. A burning ember had settled on his sleeve and burned through the material. Anthony brushed the cinder off.

Rachel shook, panic and instinct now overruling her body.

"Keep focused," he commanded.

She swore like a sailor, retrieved the last precious arrow, licking the end feathers for accuracy. After pushing the arrow into the cradle and anchoring it, she took aim and fired. The arrow sailed. The velocity and propulsion prompted by the crossbow buried the point into the tree trunk. *Clunk.* Rachel tested the rope. "It will hold our weight."

He boosted her up onto a high ledge and clambered up next to her, standing, unsteady on the precipice. From the windows below, smoke billowed. Tongues of fire pitched skyward.

She coughed. Her eyes watered. Beneath them, far beneath them, the lawns spread out to the forest, beckoning like a tranquil oasis. To have more time. But they were out of time.

Through the waving smoke he peered. Cuthbert was nowhere. Must have been satisfied his mission was accomplished, and he decided to leave before the townspeople saw the fire.

"This will work," he affirmed.

She closed her eyes...and swayed.

"Do you have a fear of heights?"

"A little. Can't think about that now."

Anthony slid the block out. Energy shot through him. She called to the dog. Casey leapt in her arms. Anthony sat on the roped chair, held Rachel, and she held the dog.

One. Two. Three.

The next seconds blurred, whooshing through the air, Rachel's hair flying in his face, and the rope bowing with their weight. Would the arrow hold? Anthony stretched his long legs forward... slammed into the tree, grabbed a branch and steadied their rocking.

"How good are you at climbing down trees?" Anthony asked.

Rachel scrambled onto the branch, the dog gave a little bark and Anthony joined them.

"I'm a Colonial. But don't tell me Colonials are born in trees. Difficult with the dog and this dress." She handed the dog to Anthony and bent over to tear her skirt off.

"Now there's a thought."

"Don't get any ideas." She tied her skirts into a pouch. Anthony put the dog in, slung the sack over his shoulder. The dog whined. "Don't look down. One branch at a time."

The next seconds improved, descending the tree, testing each limb to see if it held his weight and making sure Rachel followed the correct footholds. On the ground, he released the dog, and then reached up and caught Rachel in his arms. "I'm never letting you go."

"Well, Well."

Anthony put her down and spun around. Cuthbert and his four henchmen, their faces like grinning demons in the firelight. A gun leveled at Anthony's chest. A callous, predatory enjoyment fired inside Anthony. "You're going to require more than that."

Cuthbert sneered. "I have the gun."

A vein pulsed in Anthony's forehead. "You better make it count because none of you are going to last."

The thugs tittered.

"Wrist," Rachel commanded. The dog leaped, grinding her teeth into Cuthbert's arm, and dangled from his sleeve. The gun went off, landed somewhere in the leaves. Twigs and splinters showered on their heads. Anthony sprang into action. The thugs fell on him and he roared out an awful challenge. He punched one in the nose, making a popping sound, and dousing him in a shower of blood. With lightening quick ease, Anthony broke free and swung his elbow into a man's windpipe. The thug emitted a shuddering breath and pitched backward. They backed off. Not surprising. These were not seasoned fighters. Two down, three to go. He'd been looking for a fight. His eyes fixed on his prey.

One huge thug grew brave, plowed at Anthony like the prow of a ship, slamming him in the jaw. Stunned, Anthony grasped one of the huge wrists and broke it in two. He stopped and hit the next man with a colossal right. All the way up from his planted feet, as hard as he could and felt his fist drive right through it and beyond it. His falling body weight whipped his head out from under his moving hand. The momentum allowed him to carry onward, shoulder first into the thug who got hit in the windpipe.

He faced Cuthbert. "Come on, you coward," Anthony taunted, springing sinuously to one side and then to another. He wanted to finish this.

Cuthbert's lips pulled back from his teeth. He charged Anthony, aiming a savage blow at the head, which if it had landed, would have crushed Anthony's skull. He danced to the side, dropping beneath it, delivered with a clenched fist, a mighty blow himself into the pit of the rogue's stomach. He kicked Cuthbert between the legs, and the man's head jerked downward at the same time Anthony's elbow jerked upward, doubling the power of the blow. Cuthbert face-flopped into the moldy leaves.

Anthony wiped his bloody knuckles on Cuthbert's dirty shirt. "I told you, you needed more men."

Rachel flew into his arms. Shouts echoed from the woods behind them. "My father's coming with his guards. You didn't think I'd come here alone, did you?" He scratched his head. "Why they have come so late is a mystery."

She spread her petticoats to show her indecent attire. "Oh, dear. Your father is coming, and I'm clad like this?"

Anthony laughed, took his coat off and draped it over her shoulders. "You endured a burning house, flying fifty feet above the ground, and you're worried about your state of dress?"

The duke arrived with several armed groomsmen, guards, Captain Johnson and curious townspeople.

Anthony stroked his jaw where he'd been hit and looked at his father. "What took you so long?"

"Went to the wrong sea captain's house. You didn't specify." At the Duke's nod, they tied up the villains, yanked a groggy Cuthbert up on his feet. "You will be facing a hanging," said the Duke.

Cuthbert spat. "You think so? There are more of us and you'll never see them coming. We may have missed getting Lady Abigail but we did get Lord Nicolas. Too bad his ship went down." Cuthbert started coughing with that coal dust laugh. The crowd buzzed.

The Duke held up his hand to silence everyone. "Who?" demanded the Duke.

The sea captain's house exploded, and then collapsed, shooting flames to the sky as the last of the wood structure was consumed by flames. A shot rang out from the west side of the inferno. Anthony covered Rachel with his body, hitting the ground hard. Who the hell was shooting? Everyone scrambled.

"Guards, search the woods," the duke demanded.

Cuthbert slumped. Blood poured from his chest, shot in the heart. Anthony felt Cuthbert's pulse, his split lip curled with disgust. There were no more shots. Anthony rose, pulled Rachel up. The duke came up beside him. "Dead. Obviously who did this, did not want Cuthbert to reveal the scoundrel. Now we'll never know."

Chapter 18

A fire blazed in the hearth, warming Rachel. They were all together in the library, Anthony's father, Aunt Margaret, the constable, Anthony, the Duke of Westbrook, and Sebastian, who stood in front of the closed doors.

The Duke of Westbrook leaned against the mantle, indolent, savoring a sip of his brandy. He licked his lips like a cat fed a bowl of warm milk, surprising everyone with his presence. "It is too bad you were unable to confront Cuthbert Noot."

Over the rim of her teacup, Rachel studied the Rutland's close family friend. How odd his formal dress at this late hour. His clothing fit well, his wig faultlessly brushed and powdered, yet there was an expression of strained politeness in his manner.

"What a pack of rats," said Anthony's father. "We rounded up the rest of the criminals. Nothing was gleaned from them. Cuthbert had the only interface with the scoundrel who has schemed this wicked madness."

"So clever of you to have escaped." Cornelius Westbrook stared at Anthony, his manner almost accusing.

Stop overreacting. Hadn't Cornelius availed himself at every disaster to help the Rutland's in fighting their dreadful enemies? Didn't he insist on rebuilding Anthony's laboratory after it had exploded? Anthony and his father seemed unperturbed. Why should she be bothered?

"Terrible circumstances...to be burned alive." Anthony's father shook his head. "To think you outsmarted Cuthbert—the crossbow, the block and tackle, the flight over ground."

Anthony sat next to her on the settee, the dog on his lap, his other arm perched behind, touched her shoulder. "All the credit goes to Rachel and Casey. Rachel's ability with the crossbow and Casey's loyalty." The dog lifted her head at the sound of her name and Anthony rubbed behind the canine's ears. "Casey will have fresh meat for her dinner until the end of time."

"And to think you thought Casey was without wit," Rachel reminded him.

"Never. This is the smartest dog this side of the Atlantic." Casey rolled her head to have him scratch behind her other ear.

Did Cornelius's glass eye turn blacker or was it a trick of the light? Shark black. Rachel stopped smiling.

The Duke of Westbrook tipped his glass and bottomed out his brandy. "I cannot think of the horror you both faced. To have the next Rutland heir destroyed."

Rachel stiffened. Was that a veiled threat? Anthony leaned against the back of the settee with unstudied negligence, listening, saying no word but watching Cornelius. Was Anthony suspicious too?

"Providential you were able to keep your faculties," said Anthony's father to them still mystified at their survival.

"Very fortunate," Cornelius smiled engagingly.

Anger. Definitely anger. A knot grew in her belly. What might have been spoken graciously was condemning.

The Constable clapped his hands on his knees and rose. "We must find out who shot Noot. We searched the woods. Disappointing, the rascal disappeared."

"How timely, Noot was shot before he could speak," said the duke.

"Fortunate for Mrs. Noot to not to have to live in terror of her husband resurfacing," Rachel said unable to tear her eyes away from Cornelius.

The constable headed for the doors. "We've got enough for one evening. I will continue with the investigation to see what I can ferret out. As before, I'm sorry we've come up with dead ends, Your Grace."

Cornelius set his glass on the mantle. "I must leave. I received a message to return home. I will use my resources to look into the matter as best I can."

"Thank you." Anthony's father shook his old friend's hand and the man departed.

"Remarkable Duke Cornelius's visit so late at night, father."

"Nothing unusual. He had sent word two weeks ago that he was planning to visit, arrived at the time of the commotion, insisting on joining us."

If only she could pull Anthony aside. Wasn't Cornelius nearby when Abby and Nicolas were abducted and when the lab blew up?

Anthony nodded and stood. "With that settled, I'd like to speak to Miss Thorne—alone."

Rachel gaped.

The Duke of Rutland nodded his assent and escorted the reticent, Aunt Margaret, who dodged a wink at her, and Sebastian closed the doors behind them.

Anthony knelt in front of her and her heart went to her throat. "I think I know what you are going to say, but—"

He pressed two fingers on her lips. "You will listen and let me voice what I need to say." His blue eyes were breathtaking in their intensity, deep sapphire blue. "I love how you drag me out in the cold and snow, making me aware of the simplest things that I've long taken for granted. I love how you wind your hair around your finger when you are thinking. I love how you temper my strong-willed nature, putting me back on track and pointing the right way with my experiments. I love how that brain of yours works. I love that after I spend the day with you, I can still smell your lemon and lavender scent on my clothes. I've been lonely all my life and now realize when you meet someone that is the person you want to spend the rest of your life with, you want it to begin as soon as possible."

Unshed tears scalded her eyes, coming deep from the soul's well. The greatest treasure of her life, she'd have to give up. There was a disturbance in the hall, but Rachel was wound so tight with emotion, the commotion seemed a million miles away. Silence filled the room and the time seemed never-ending. Her body shook with the strain, ripping her insides.

She stroked his hair, swallowing an upsurge of sobs. "That was the most beautiful proposal any woman could have been offered, Anthony. But I cannot marry you."

He frowned, the confusion in his mind flashed across his face. "Why? Tell me you don't love me."

She swallowed hard, not trusting her voice. "It's because I love you, Anthony, I'm turning you down. You are the heir, the next Duke of Rutland. I am a Colonial, far from the pedigree you need to have at your side. I am unable to fill those shoes. Your family would forbid it."

"Pedigree be damned. I don't care what anyone thinks. I want you, Rachel."

"You are not thinking clearly. I will go. You will find someone who suits you."

He stood up holding her hands. "You are a woman who is bent on pleasing others. As long as everyone around you is happy you pretend all is well, concealing your despair and guilt while supporting the wretched status quo to reject your true desire. Let me make you happy."

She pulled to free her hands from his, but he held firm.

"If I become duke, the well-being of the tenants and the estate depend on my sound judgment. If my brother returns, I will need help and a clear head to continue my experiments. All those things depend on my state of happiness. I could never be happy without you, Rachel, and I want to have a family with you."

"No, Anthony." She shook her head, trapped in a lonely world, a longing for connection, a hidden cry to be possessed. *Impossible.* "I'll be leaving within the week."

"Then I'm forced to do something to prevent you."

Rachel froze. "What are you going to do?"

He strode to the door, yanked it open. In fell Aunt Margaret, clutching her swaying ear horn to her chest. Anthony's father straightened his waistcoat. Behind them, Sebastian inspected an area of the ceiling that suddenly needed his scrutiny. Rachel put her hands on her cheeks. They had heard every word.

Anthony looked them dead in the eye. "I have compromised Miss Thorne and she *will* marry me."

Dying from the mortification over what they had heard was bad enough, but this added humiliation? All she could do was stare at Anthony. He'd gone mad. Oh, to pound every unpredictable bone in his body.

The duke spoke. "I will correct one misconception, Miss Thorne. You will be a *very* welcomed addition to the family. I would be very proud to have you as a daughter-in-law."

Aunt Margaret tottered closer, planting herself next to Rachel before she could bolt. "You will marry Anthony." She leaned in, spoke low and confidingly. "We could discuss the bath in the new bathtub and the day spent out in the laboratory—alone."

Rachel widened her eyes. "You wouldn't." How wily the old woman was.

"I would," confirmed Aunt Margaret. "We want you to stay."

"Before we go any further," Anthony said, pointedly looking at his aunt's ear horn. "Do you really need that contraption?"

She puffed herself up like a peacock. "Of course not. For someone so smart, my feigned deafness took you long enough to figure out." She waved a hand dismissively, and then pivoted to Rachel. "Abby sent you here for Anthony. It was her plan. The duke, and I, with a little help from Sebastian, created an environment where two extraordinary and lonely souls who were meant for each other had time to develop a romance. If you want to blame anyone, blame Abby, but she had both of your hearts in mind."

That these three knew all along? That they had conspired with Abby and they wanted her as part of their family? Rachel turned and blubbered into Anthony's shirt. His strong arms automatically enclosed her.

He held her face in his hands. "You haven't answered me. Will you marry me?"

"Oh Anthony, you are the light of my heart. Yes. A thousand times, yes."

Epilogue

The last six weeks had been a whirlwind. Anthony insisted on a small wedding and that the marriage take place right away, and if it could not be done, then he was kidnapping her to Gretna Green. Under great pressure, the Duke, Aunt Margaret and the house staff pulled magic from the air to make a semi-small wedding occur. Rachel smiled, semi-small translated to five hundred guests.

She was sad that her family could not have attended. How she missed Jacob, Abby and the baby. Impossible with the distances, the war, and with Abby expecting again. Arranged by the Duke of Banfield, Ethan had been smuggled in from Lisbon for the ceremony, delighting her, and giving her away.

Now that the celebration was over, they enjoyed a brief honeymoon in Wales. The bitter chill of January had eclipsed and the promise of Spring came with the warm sun slanting across the bed. When they returned, they would take up residence in Belvoir Castle. It would have been unconscionable for them to take up residence elsewhere, protested the Duke and Aunt Margaret although Rachel suspected they didn't want to be alone. The only bad reflection was the onerous chore of the dukedom casting a shadow over Anthony's head. He was made for science not administrative work.

The clock in the hall struck twelve times. Midday. Sinful how they had not yet risen from bed. Rachel snuggled up to Anthony, running her toes along his leg. "Are you awake?"

"How can I not be when I have to meet my wife's insatiable needs."

She looked up at him, her heart bursting with love, the terrible poverty of loneliness wiped clean from their lives. "What are you thinking?"

"Biology. The first time on the cot in my laboratory was two months ago, plus seven more months equals a complete gestation period. Are you?"

"You are a sly thing. Did Mrs. Noot—"

"I'm a scientist. I have an exact formula for everything, coupled with the usual signs— nausea, fatigue, emotion."

"I am not emotional." She pinched his chin, and then reached over to the end table, letting her breasts, fuller now, deliberately trail across his chest. He moaned and hardened beneath her. Predictable.

She straddled him, wriggling her bottom just so, to taunt him, picked up a gold embossed envelope and read it for the hundredth time. "The Most Honorable, The Marquess of Rutland, has been invited to the Royal Society of Science esteemed for his work in electricity and elected for life through a peer review process on the basis of excellence in science."

She flopped back on the pillows, folding the letter and placing it in the envelope, smiling because she had created a thirst in her swaggering husband that would have to be slaked. He dropped soft kisses on her face and throat, meeting her lips in a searing demanding kiss. He cupped her swollen breasts, spilling heavily into his hands, scraping lightly over her rigid nipples with his thumbs until she moaned. She reached up and pulled him down to her, stunned by the force of the pulsating need in him, and gasped, accepting his thick fullness. Thrill after thrill shot through her as he possessed her body, buried so deep inside it made her hunger for him all the more.

She pressed a kiss against the pulse in his neck.

"I love you with everything I am, and everything I ever will be. Body, mind, heart, soul," he said, and hauled her up against him. How she cherished the steady beat of his heart against her ear, and his warm musk, lingering in the air. Her hands ran over his damp skin. He stopped her.

"You are a vixen, wife. We should have twins when you are done with me."

Would she survive if she surrendered to the craving she saw in the smoldering depths of his eyes?

Before the question was answered, a knock sounded at the door. "What is it?" Anthony bellowed. Her husband would not be disturbed on his honeymoon.

He tore the sheet from the bed, wrapped it around his midsection and threw open the door. The maid stuttered, thrusting a missive into his hands. Anthony slammed the door. Rachel would have to work on his manners.

She sat up, alarmed with the intensity with which he read the letter. "Is it bad news?"

"On the contrary. My father has written and wants us home. Nicholas is alive."

Author's Note

During the eighteenth century there was enormous work with electricity by great scientists, including, Dr. Benjamin Franklin, Luigi Galvani and Alessandro Volta.

In 1752, Dr. Benjamin Franklin conducted his experiment with a kite, a key, and a storm. This demonstrated that lightning and small electric sparks were identical. Franklin's discovery indicated that the generation of a positive charge tied-in with the generation of an equal negative charge, otherwise known as the law of conservation of change—a key scientific breakthrough. Franklin's results showed the single-fluid theory of electricity. He experimented with arresting and storing electrical charges, utilizing, the Leyden jar, a primitive form of capacitor. His experimentation led to a new device that he named the electrical battery. Dr. Franklin was admitted to the esteemed Royal Society for his work.

In 1780, Luigi Galvani discovered that the muscles of dead frogs' legs twitched when struck by an electrical spark. His work was one of the initial ventures into the examination of bioelectricity, a discipline that remains, searching the patterns and signals of the nervous system.

In 1800, Italian physicist Alessandro Volta invented the voltaic pile, an improved electric battery that generated a steady electric current. Volta concluded that the greatest effective pair of dissimilar metals produced electricity. He initiated a series of experiment using zinc, lead, tin and iron as positive plates (cathode): and copper, silver, gold and graphite as negative plates (anode). The interest in electricity soon became prevalent.

In *Light of My Heart*, I took artistic license, and said, *what if*—I blend the unique breakthroughs of Dr. Franklin and Alessandro Volta into the experimentation and discoveries of Anthony Rutland and Rachel Thorne. A delightful story unfolded...

About the Author

Elizabeth St. Michel is the award-winning and bestselling author of *The Winds of Fate*, for which she was a quarter-finalist for the Amazon Breakthrough Novel Award and was a number one hit on the Amazon bestseller lists.

Her second novel, *Surrender the Wind*, won Toronto's "the Catherine," Washington, D.C.'s "the Marlene," Virginia's prestigious Holt Medallion, InD'tale's, Crowned Heart, and finalist for the famed National RONE Award in honor of literary excellence in romance writing. Born and raised in Western New York, she is the mother of five wonderful children.

Acknowledgements

Most books wouldn't be written without the help of some special people. I would like to acknowledge Caroline Tolley, my developmental editor and Linda Style, my copy/line editor. Their insight and expertise were indispensable. Hugs also to my spouse, Edward, five children, eight grandchildren, Dr. Marcianna Dollard, Nancy Crawford, and posthumously, Loretta Bysiek—your love and comfort surround me.

Many thanks to the gracious support of Western New York Romance Writers Group.

Finally, a special note of gratitude to my readers. You will never know how much your enthusiasm and support enrich my work and my life. You are the best.

Dear Readers,

It has given me particular pleasure to write, *Light of My Heart* for you. There is no greater compliment to me as an author than for my readers to become so involved with the characters that you want me to write more. That said, I'm happily immersed in a series with the powerful Duke of Rutland, a widower, and his four strong-willed offspring. As you know, my first installment, *Sweet Vengeance* detailed the journey of Abigail, his only daughter and the notorious privateer, Jacob Thorne during the American Revolution.

My second installment, *Light of My Heart* acquaints us with Abby's older brother, Anthony Rutland, a hopeless introvert, and brilliant scientist who wants nothing to do except work in his laboratory. Abigail sends Rachel Thorne, Jacob's cousin to her ancestral home in England to be introduced into society. How unfortunate, for Anthony to have his quiet world turned upside down by the spirited Rachel and even worse, with an intellect to match. But there are still enemies intent on destroying the Rutland family...

My third in the series centers around Nicholas, the eldest son and heir of the Duke of Rutland. Kidnapped and thrown onto a Brazilian slaver, he makes the unlikely friendship with an enigmatic woman of no heritage. Their ship splits apart during a hurricane and both are tossed on a deserted island where they must work together to survive. But soon his desire for her sparks into a wildfire of passion, he can no longer deny and they must risk confronting their dangerous pasts for a chance at a future in each other's arms.

Although I can't tell you much more I can promise you this: like my last novels, it is written with one goal in mind—to make you experience the laughter, the love, and all the other myriad emotions of its characters. And when it's over to leave you smiling...

Warmly,
Elizabeth St. Michel

P.S. If you would like to receive an emailed newsletter from me, which will keep you informed about my books-in-progress as well as answer some of the questions I'm frequently asked about publishing, please contact me on Facebook or my webpage at elizabethstmichel.com. The greatest gift you can give an author is a review for her work on the website you have purchased the book. I would be thrilled to hear from you!

CPSIA information can be obtained
at www.ICGtesting.com
Printed in the USA
BVHW031944120921
616628BV00012B/79